About the Author

Graham Oxley was born in 1945 in Weston-Super-Mare and, aside from a year of hitchhiking around Europe in his late teens, has lived there for his entire life.

He went to the local grammar school and left at the age of seventeen with two O-levels to his name. His academic failure at school might have been due to the fact that his mother became ill when he was about seven years old. She died of cancer when he was nine years old. He likes to think that the lack of her guiding hand through his school years was the reason he did not pass exams. However, he does concede that it was probably due to his own laziness and his failure to ever do any homework which caused him to leave school with no qualifications.

He worked at a variety of jobs after leaving school but never found anything which he really liked. Instead, he began studying at home and eventually gained a law degree at a local college. Finally, after several years, he qualified as a solicitor and ended up practising in his home town for about twenty years, before retiring at the age of sixty-nine. It was only then that he began writing seriously and was able to find the time to finish the novel which he had started writing about fifty years before. It's never too late.

Covid Injustice

Graham Oxley

Covid Injustice

Vanguard Press

VANGUARD PAPERBACK

© Copyright 2024
Graham Oxley

The right of Graham Oxley to be identified as author of
this work has been asserted by him in accordance with the
Copyright, Designs and Patents Act 1988.

All Rights Reserved

No reproduction, copy or transmission of this publication
may be made without written permission.
No paragraph of this publication may be reproduced,
copied or transmitted save with the written permission of the
publisher, or in accordance with the provisions
of the Copyright Act 1956 (as amended).

Any person who commits any unauthorised act in relation to
this publication may be liable to criminal
prosecution and civil claims for damages.

A CIP catalogue record for this title is
available from the British Library.

ISBN 978 1 83794 181 0

This is a work of fiction. Names, characters, businesses, places, events and
incidents are either the product of the author's imagination or used in a
fictitious manner. Any resemblance to actual persons, living or dead, or actual
events is purely coincidental.

Vanguard Press is an imprint of
Pegasus Elliot Mackenzie Publishers Ltd.
www.pegasuspublishers.com

First Published in 2024

Vanguard Press
Sheraton House Castle Park
Cambridge England

Printed & Bound in Great Britain

For all doctors and nurses in hospitals, health centres and anyone who helped e.g. in doctor's surgeries.

Chapter 1

Abbigail, who had worked now in a legal office for more than six months, had grown used to wearing a face mask at work. In the offices of 'Featherstones' solicitors the manager, Mr Morris, had always thought that the wearing of masks was essential both for public health and for the individual protection of his staff.

At the start of the pandemic there was more insistence that masks should be worn everywhere but later there were less stringent rules and regulations and often people felt as if it was entirely up to the individual whether he or she wore one.

Abbigail was OK with that, but she had found that mask wearing was not quite as straight forward as she had supposed. Her kind -hearted mother had made her several masks which she expected her daughter to wear whenever she was out and about. That was all very well but Abbie found that the material her mother had used was a design she recognized from her mother's sewing basket and which she remembered was left over from a pair of pyjamas her mother had made for her about twenty-five years ago. Regrettably the material pictured many small Donald Ducks cavorting about in the snow. She did not wish to wear such a mask but did not care to advise her mother of her feeling. She realized that she would have to wear one of the masks whenever she was meeting her mother. Also, she knew because her mother had made several similar masks, that she would not be able to pretend that she had lost one of them.

She accepted that she would have to wear one of her mother's masks if\she was meeting her, but she was too embarrassed to ever wear one to the office. She had purchased an ordinary plain white one for that purpose. She knew that her mother probably felt that anyone who saw the Donald Duck mask would regard it as cute, but Abbigail did not. She could not understand why her own mother continued to treat her as if she were still about six years old. She presumed that the era when she was about that age was her mother's favourite time and that probably as the years had passed, her mother had refused to keep up with the progress of Abbie's development. She wondered how many mothers there were with the same attitude.

Abbie's mother was called Stephanie and when she was a young girl, she had looked like Abbie looked now. If boys passed her in the street, they would turn and look a second time and purse their lips in appreciation of her beauty. They would watch as her legs and bottom disappeared up the street.

Now, in the forty ninth year of her life Stephanie no longer attracted such admiration from the males in the street. Her frame over the years had filled out into the shape of a large pear. Her complexion had acquired the appearance of a mature apple or pear, a pale pink shade tinged with a more scarlet spot on each cheek. She now had the appearance of 'Mrs Bun' the baker's wife. She had always been talented and innovative with her needle and thread and her sewing machine which her husband had given to her to celebrate one of their wedding anniversaries. She had quickly run up the Covid face masks, some of which she had donated to her daughter, and others which she had circulated around the family. Abbie's elder brother had deposited his mask in the bin whereas her father dutifully donned his Donald duck mask each time he left the house. Ironically, he even wore it when he was going outside to occupy his potting shed in the garden, presumably in case he should encounter someone therein. What perplexed and mildly outraged Abbie most of all was that her mother had made a single special mask which she herself wore. This one was made from a pink paisley material and her daughter was convinced that this single separate article said everything that needed to be said about the Donald duck masks.

Since the pandemic had occurred, life for the whole family had changed considerably. Abbie who was in her mid-twenties, still lived at home with her mother and father. Her brother who was three years older than her, was married and lived about three miles away with his wife and two-year-old baby boy. If anything, his life had been altered the least in the family. He worked in the building industry and was as busy now as he had been before the disease first emerged from the other side of the world. He worked each day on an empty building site without contact with anyone except the other members of his gang on site. No members of the public came to the site and each day, when he finished his work, he went home to his wife and child. For the first year of the epidemic, they purchased all their food and other supplies online and spent all their time watching their baby grow up.

Abbie on the other hand found that her life had been altered considerably by the arrival of Covid. Her social activities had dried up. With the closure of bars and night clubs, her habitual way of meeting others, especially boys, had ended. She had not had a date with a man for about fourteen months, nor had she any way of meeting any. She had therefore made the decision to sign up with an online dating site, something she had never done before. She knew that such sites were now very popular and much favoured by youngsters such as herself. Although she was aware of this, she had always felt that she had never found any difficulty in attracting a man before and therefore viewed such sites previously with some contempt or even pity. She felt perhaps that they were used primarily by older people who had perhaps already missed the boat.

She had a chat with a close friend Joyce with whom she had been at school and who lived nearby and who was one of the few regular friends that were available to her. Joyce advised her that her opinion of dating sites was behind the times.

"Everyone does it now," she said, and immediately offered to assist her to make out her profile for the site which Abbie was already struggling with.

"No not like that," she said, altering almost all the entries which Abbie had already entered.

"It is not necessary to tell the complete truth on most of the entries. Hardly anyone ever does. Never," she said emphatically. "Tell the truth about your age."

She deducted five years from Abbie's age entry and where Abbie had entered 'looking for a serious relationship' she re-entered the words 'looking for fun and pleasure'. Abbie said she was not sure about that, but Joyce insisted that she knew what she was doing.

"If you say what you wrote, you'll end up with some sad old man who already has one foot in the grave."

Abbie left her to it and did not interfere over any of the other entries. Joyce quickly completed the entries and pressed the 'send' button and waited for the machine to absorb all the details and produce the results on the screen. Abbie had previously intended to attach a photograph of herself riding a bicycle along a woodland path which her mother had taken a year before. Joyce poo pooed this and instead took a picture with her smart phone of Abbie standing in the bathroom in her bra and pants.

"Try to look provocative," she urged, and Abbie tried to do so but was not confident.

They ended up with a profile that looked, to Joyce, very impressive and inviting. Abbie was not so sure. Her photograph looked to her as if she had been taken by surprise in the middle of her toilet which was an appearance which she really did not care for.

Once her application or entry was completed, they both waited to see how her profile would be accepted by male applicants.

"How long is it supposed to take?" asked Abbie impatiently.

"I don't know" replied Joyce. "It's a bit like going fishing. Sometimes you can sit here all day and not get a bite whereas on a different day you may be inundated with responses. You know they say a watched kettle never boils; it is wiser to switch off and go away and bake a cake or something and come back to it tomorrow. Otherwise, it will drive you mad."

Abbie was still not confidant.

"Are you sure that it is OK to give incorrect information? I mean, when one finally meets up with someone else on a date it will be obvious that I am older than my profile states. What happens then?"

"Well, nothing at all," said Joyce, drawing on all her experience of operating on a site like this. "None of the guys take the trouble to read the profiles meticulously. And in any case, virtually all the blokes lie in their profiles."

"Do you really think so?" asked Abbie. "Aren't there any honest ones out there?"

"Hardly ever," confirmed her friend. "How many of the guys on this site do you suppose are married? At least fifty per cent I would guess but if you look through all the profiles on here, I bet you won't find a single one who admits to being married."

"Really?" said Abbie in astonishment. "But what, if that is the case are they doing here on this site?"

"Well," replied Joyce with absolute confidence. "Most or all of them are looking for casual sex."

"Really?" responded Abbey with much disappointment in her voice. But that is not really what I am looking for. I was hoping to find a nice-looking young man with a sense of humour with whom I could have some fun dates. I am not looking for a stud after all and certainly not a married one. How is one supposed to separate the wheat from the chaff when some replies are received?"

Joyce was non-specific, "Well, it's just a case of getting a feel for them all. That is part of what makes sites like this interesting. You never know who you may end up with. You could either get a glamorous film star type or a Caliban."

"What's a Caliban?" queried Abbie.

"Don't you remember, the character in the Tempest that we had to study at school. The half-man, half-monster creature created by Shakespeare. I don't think Mr Lewis our English Lit teacher would be pleased to discover that you had forgotten his instruction periods."

Abbie gave a slight shudder as if she had felt someone walking across her grave.

"That's another thing," she said. "Isn't there some danger in delving into this sort of thing online?"

"None whatsoever," responded Joyce. "That's the beauty of this sort of site. You can say or do whatever you like. No one will be able to stalk or molest or compromise you at all so long as you do not give away any personal information."

"But," said Abbie warily. "What about when you agree to meet up with anyone you meet on this site? You are no longer safe then, are you?"

"Ahh," said Joyce with some admittance. "There's the rub of course. But then you are in the same situation as the good old days on any first date. You must trust your instincts and be very careful who you choose."

"So, despite all the assurances and persuasive arguments, these sorts of sites are not safe at all unless you decide never to meet anyone in person?"

"Um," agreed Joyce with reservation. "That is true, but while there are all sorts of danger out there in this Covid infested world, it is surely better to enjoy some fun and flirting in complete security."

Abbie was flabbergasted by this, "Are you saying that it is better never to meet anyone from this site when going on a date? Have you ever met anyone from this site who is in any way attractive or worth knowing?"

"Well," said Joyce with care. "I have met many men virtually and a great many of them have been very exciting and satisfying."

"But have you actually met a single man as a result of chatting online?"

"Hmm," replied Joyce again with reservation. "I haven't actually met anyone yet, but the possibility is always there and that, is exciting. It's like buying a lottery ticket, isn't it? Just being on this sort of site is excitement in itself."

"Is it?" asked Abbie, with some scepticism, and wondered vaguely what manner of replies she would receive.

Chapter 2

Abbie's parents, Mr and Mrs Wilson had been married now for thirty years. They were the epitome of a happily married respectable couple. He was a retired accountant who had worked for years with the local authority where he had met his wife who had worked as a computer operator in a different department. As a retired couple they were financially secure. Both received a generous works pension from their ex-employer, and each had also contributed to a private pension. In addition, both were only children whose parents had already died and passed on to their respective children a sizeable inheritance. They lived in a generous four-bedroomed house for which the mortgage had long ago been paid off and drove a comfortable German estate car.

Neither of their children had been told or would ever have guessed that when they were much younger, their mother and father used to visit pop concerts regularly and used to smoke marijuana when they were there. They had attended the very first Glastonbury concert and had met Michael Eavis when they were there. They considered themselves to be both liberal and culturally advanced. Abbie's father read the Guardian every day. He convinced himself that this kept him young in spirit. He had been thinking for a long time to grow himself a small pigtail at the back of his head, but his now grey hair did not seem to grow as quickly as it used to. His wife had stopped colouring her hair and was now allowing her natural grey hair to come through. Despite their physical appearance they both regarded themselves as young and vibrant and occasionally Mr Wilson still idly considered the concept of wife swapping but admittedly now, he did not entertain these thoughts so often.

Since the advent of the Covid pandemic their social life had been curtailed considerably. Mr Wilson's golf activities had ceased and so too had his wife's yoga sessions. They existed almost entirely in their own house, rarely venturing out for any reason other than to stock up on petrol to run their car in which they would visit close family. They regularly saw their grandson Rupert as often as possible but despite their eagerness they found that their contact with him was dwindling. Their daughter-in-law Sheila, was rigorous with the daily contact which her family had with anyone and on each occasion of contact she would interrogate them both as to their health and, in particular, if either of them displayed signs of a slight cold or runny nose, she would curtail their contact.

Whenever Sheila curtailed their access to Rupert there followed a discussion between themselves about her reasoning and any justifications for her decision. Usually, her mother would criticize Sheila for depriving them of their access to Rupert. Her father would find himself taking Sheila's side, (even when he did not totally agree with her decision) simply to insert some fairness into the situation. This would result in an argument between them with the mother usually accusing him of, "Deliberately taking her side every time instead of mine. What sort of husband are you, Percy?"

Percy never really knew how to answer this question but knew in his heart that he did not want another dispute; he usually responded by saying something along the lines of, "No Stephanie, I am not taking her side; I am simply accepting that her reasons may be valid. I miss seeing Rupert as well, but I do think we should always make sure that our grandchild's best interests are the main priority."

Stephanie always had to agree with this point, or rather could not disagree, but she never wanted the discussion to end with that conclusion. She invariably reminded her husband that none of Sheila's arguments for disallowing access had so far been proved to have been justified. Percy always found himself to be floundering when this point was put to him. He knew that if he agreed with her on this point, her supplementary question would be, "Then why did you take her side?"

He was also aware that if on the other hand he chose to argue that there had been at least one time when Sheila had been correct, she would then have demanded that he name the occasion. Either way, he always knew that he would never win the argument that he had never wanted to be part of.

Aside from visits to see Rupert, the Wilsons rarely ventured out of the house during the epidemic. Inevitably they did not need to go out for any other social reason because their only other contact, their daughter Abbie lived with them anyway and so every day when she finished work, she would come home to them. If she were being honest with herself, she would admit that living at home with mum and dad was not too bad. The house was a decent size and nicely furnished and she had a private space in her own bedroom to which she could retire either to do work in the evenings or just to be on her own. She always felt some guilt about the amount of time she spent in her room by herself whilst pretending to be working on files which she brought home from the office. Most of the time she spent in her bedroom she was scrolling through messages on her smart phone.

Her mother did her best to make everyone as comfortable as possible by enthusiastically spending much of her time in the kitchen producing all kinds of foods which for years she had always meant to try out. Over the course of the lockdowns, she assiduously worked her way through most of her recipe books, many of which she had never previously visited. The results were sometimes greeted with surprise and amazement by Abbie and her father and at other times with less exuberance. The reason why her offerings were seldom received with equal enthusiasm by both was that Mr Wilson had a yearning for spicey Eastern food which, given the choice, he would eat every day at each mealtime. Abbey on the other hand had no liking for strong spicey foods and much preferred to eat salads and sea food. Sometimes their mother managed the problem by cooking both sorts of food on the same day to appeal to both., at the same meal. Eventually, she made a compromise by preparing multi-servings of a variety of meals and consigning some of them to the deep freezer and gradually building up a generous supply of meals for all tastes.

The supply of ready-made frozen foods despite the nutritional value they contained did not replace the pleasure which all the family experienced by going to a restaurant or bar to enjoy a family occasion or individually going out to eat with friends. Abbie would, before the advent of the Covid pandemic, regularly meet girlfriends in a bar or restaurant and enjoy a meal or snack and a chin wag with her friends. All that enjoyable social activity had been curtailed by the epidemic.

Stephanie and Percy Wilson were only too aware of the reduction of their mutual or individual social life. No golf for Percy, no yoga for Stephanie. They were confined to their home and the daytime television which they had never previously watched. Initially they were intrigued with the personable and overtly cheerful TV hosts who introduced them to an endless queue of show business celebrities who each had an interesting story of their own lifetime to tell and /or a book to sell about an episode of their own life or perhaps a story which they had dreamed up in their confinement about a character which no one else had ever thought of e g, a hungry friendly dragon who loves cooking.

For the first few weeks Stephanie and Percy were entranced by this constant form of entertainment and watched daily as the intriguing episodes unfolded. Eventually they became saturated with the regular supply of celebrities whom they gradually came to realize came into their lives on their screens with the same message. They soon became tired of hearing what their counterparts in Hollywood preferred to eat for breakfast and returned to their previous choices of entertainment which was reading a book or listening to the radio. In the end they only used their television to catch up on the daily news and the up-to-date information concerning the epidemic. Their excitement in life had been concentrated down to the number of times they saw their grandchild Rupert each day, and that depended, to some extent, upon how Sheila viewed things. She did not always see it as wholly appropriate that Rupert should visit his grandparents every day even though the child himself always loved to see them. On each visit to their house Sheila was unable to stop herself from interrogating them as to their health and enquiring as to whom they had been in contact with since she had last seen them. She would also inspect their refrigerator for its cleanliness and check the use-by dates on each item of food therein. Inevitably she would find an excuse for not allowing Rupert to stay too long and delay the next occasion of his visit

This attitude hurt Stephanie more than her husband who, although he loved Rupert, was not quite so enamoured with his grandchild as his wife. For her any day of her life which did not involve the company of her grandchild was a day wasted.

Chapter 3

Phil had lived alone for more than twenty years. The house he lived in was an ex-council house which had originally been rented by his now deceased wife Janet. She had purchased the house from the local authority under the 'Right to buy' scheme which had been introduced by Mrs Thatcher when she was Prime Minister. When she married Phil they both lived together in her house and raised their two children together until she contracted cancer and died. She left the house to him and everything else she had in her lifetime.

Phil had worked all his life as a clerk for an Insurance Company. He had never earned much money but the house they had lived in had cost only a small amount of money under the scheme and although, after they had children, Janet never worked, they managed to survive on his meagre wage. Janet died when the children were still in junior school and with great difficulty, he brought them both up and now, fifteen years after their mother's death, they were both out in the community and earning a living in the same town.

Their father was now retired from full time work, but he supplemented his retirement income by doing some part-time taxi driving. He did not do any of the late-night calls to pubs or night-clubs, but confined his driving work to the transfer of elderly passengers from home to supermarkets or the houses of friends or relatives. Not only did it give him a modest income, but it gave him the chance to see and chat with his patrons and assist them to carry their shopping to the doorstep.

He always enjoyed taking Mrs Beryl Smithers to Tesco's to do her shopping. She always asked about his children by name and would often give him a packet of sweets for them even though they were grown up and no longer children. She always hobbled to and from the store with her shopping especially if she purchased heavy things like a bag of potatoes or a large bottle of milk. She was only ever able to manage her load by using the store shopping trolly and relying upon Phil to help her transfer her load from his car to her kitchen when she got home. Walking for her was so difficult because of her painful hip which needed replacing. The hospital had promised her a replacement hip, but the procedure had been permanently postponed during the period in which the Health Service was preoccupied with patients suffering from Covid. Her hip replacement was placed permanently on the backburner, and she was in constant pain but never once complained and was always thinking of others.

Another of his regular passengers was Oswald Swann who also had more problems than most people his age. He was now in his eighties and had been in the Merchant Navy all his life and had sailed all over the world. He had never married or had a permanent home and had no living relatives. He had never been a spendthrift nor a saver and had always spent all the money he earned renting rooms in various towns in various countries around the world. After retirement he had only been able to find himself a basement flat to live in. It belonged in a tall Victorian block of flats which contained large bay windows on each floor from the ground floor upwards. The entrance to the block was a rather grand front door two steps up from the pavement. It had originally been built as a grand town house for a well-off Victorian family. All the rooms in the first three floors of the building were well appointed whereas the rooms on the top floor had no bay windows and were intended to be attic space or accommodation for servants.

Beside the impressive front door with its brass knocker in the centre, there was an uneven stone staircase with about ten steps and a black painted iron hand rail leading down to a door,(also painted black) to the basement flat which Oswald rented. The rooms therein consisted of a narrow hallway with a modestly sized lounge and a single bedroom and a toilet with a sink and a mirror. There was no kitchen for him, but he had an electric hob positioned on a table and would cook his food on that. The whole apartment was full of damp with some mould living on the walls. The atmosphere of the flat was not good for the lungs of Oswald. He had to keep buying inhalers for himself in an attempt to prevent his chest from rattling. He also had problems with his eyes which he discovered was caused by the cataracts therein. Although he had not taken medical advice he had already convinced himself that there was no chance of having his eyes fixed under the National Health and he knew only too well that he could not afford to pay privately for any such treatment.

He did not improve his general situation by choosing to smoke cigarettes. He had picked up the habit when he was in the Merchant Navy and during the time in his life when it was cheap to smoke. Because of his job he always obtained the objects which ruined his lungs free of duty and cheap as chips. After his retirement he was no longer able to afford the expensive variety of cigarettes which he smoked all his professional life. When he ceased working he made do by buying a packet of tobacco and rolling his own cigarettes by hand. He rolled each one as thin as a match and limited himself to only five or ten per day, which was more than he could afford, but despite the reduced number per day the damage to his lungs was still maintained and now the dampness of the atmosphere of his flat made his breathing more difficult.

At least once a month and sometimes twice, Ossie would take a taxi ride with Phil to the nearby town where he could visit the local Post Office to collect his old age pension money and buy some provisions for his food cupboard. Although the Post Office and shops were no more than five miles away Oswald was not able to comfortably manage the walk without frequently stopping to draw breath. The local bus service was both unreliable and infrequent. On route they chatted away and Oswald told Phil about all the places he had visited during his life in the Merchant Navy.

Chapter 4

Abbigail had delayed going online to review the replies, if any, to the dating site profile which she had offered. She had left it for one full day upon the advice of her good friend Joyce. Twenty-four hours later Joyce called round to see her again, and as soon as they were both upstairs in her bedroom the laptop was switched on and Abbie logged on to the dating site to see what responses if any awaited her.

She was shocked and amazed to find how many replies she had received. The first received in time was from a middle-aged man in Birmingham who was entitled Hercules. Abbie was slightly confused at the man's name and said so to Joyce who explained that it was entirely normal for entrants to use non de plumes. The man himself had attached a photograph of himself which revealed a heavily built man dressed in a pair of speedo's whose body had an unlikely orange colour and which must clearly have been obtained from a bottle. He was also flexing his biceps in a manner which presumably he fondly supposed was reminiscent of the original Hercules. His body was shining from what appeared to be the application of oil all over him .Abbie could not even bring herself to read the message which he had sent her. With a shudder she had immediately pressed the delete button much to the disappointment of her friend who had wanted to read the message.

"You should never delete before reading the message she insisted. Photographs can sometimes be misleading, one can only judge someone properly by comparing the photo with the message."

Abbie was sceptical, "Well I think he looked weird and I don't care what sort of message he wrote, I could never contemplate having anything to do with him."

The second message in time was from someone who called himself 'Chip the chippie' and his picture showed him to be wearing a pair of workman's boots with a pair of black shorts and a workman's belt which contained several tools including a hammer, screwdriver and saw. Before Abbie could delete his entry Joyce took over to scroll down to read his descriptive profile. He lived in Dorchester apparently and enclosed a second picture which showed some timber decking which he assured the reader that he had laid outside his own house. In his profile he had entered in the 'Looking for' section, 'A customer with benefits'. He sported a large bushy beard which Abbie did not like the look of similar to the members of the band ZZ Top. Joyce was also unimpressed with his appearance and outraged at his impudence in trying to combine dating information with commercial gain. By mutual consent Chip's entry was deleted.

The next candidate called himself Pete eighty-one. They both presumed that eighty-one was his birth date which made him almost forty years old which made him fifteen years older than Abbie. She, for her part, had no objection to teaming up with a man who was older than her but in her mind that older man would have to be worth the effort. On first sight Pete was not very good looking and in his 'occupation ' section of his profile he had stated that he was an accountant whose overwhelming interest in life was steam engines. His profile also stated that he was looking earnestly for a girl with similar interests. Abbigail's main interests were long walks in the countryside and listening to pop music which in no way matched those of Pete, so with very little reluctance his entry page was deleted.

Abbie and Joyce moved on to the next visitor to her site. This visitor was younger than the first three by the look of him. He also had a number next to his name and his number was eighty-nine which seemed to indicate that he was possibly nearly ten years younger than Pete who had just been deleted. This man's name or title was Cotswold Traveller eighty-nine. He was apparently a civil servant and he enjoyed music and hiking. He had also revealed that he sometimes wrote poetry. This was enough to persuade both of them to examine this man's page more closely.

The message he left said, "I am so pleased to be able to speak to you and hope to be hiking with you across the Cotswolds with which I am totally familiar and will be pleased to point out to you all the famous spots."

"Hmm," said Abbie who had not expected a message of that kind. She did not really know what she had expected but had to admit to herself that she was not looking forward to a guided tour of the Cotswolds. Joyce thought it was quite romantic and suggested that she write a message back to him.

"But what shall I say to him?" she asked.

"Oh, I don't know," replied Joyce. "Tell him what sort of man you are looking for and what you would like to do if you were together."

"OK," said Abbie and wrote an entry into her laptop telling the reader that she did not live in the Cotswolds nor was she particularly interested in seeing that countryside. She told him that she was more interested in remaining in her town and walking in her nearby park and listening to music. They waited for about ten minutes and then received a reply from the Cotswold traveller who said, "Where exactly do you live? What sort of music do you listen to?"

"Well, go on, tell him," ordered Joyce. "Answer his question why don't you ."

"What you mean give him my exact address?" asked Abbie incredulously.

"No, of course not," replied Joyce irritably. "Just tell him you come from Bristol, don't tell him your precise address stupid."

Abbigail did not care for the way Joyce had spoken to her but managed to retain enough savoir faire to write another message confirming her hometown as Bristol and advising him that she was fond of Little Mix. Soon after came a further reply from the Cotswold traveller stating that he had never heard of Little Mix and that Bristol was further than he was prepared to travel. Abbie found this so annoying that she immediately pressed the delete button and that was the end of the Cotswold traveller.

"Well," said Joyce blandly. "That went well."

"I know," agreed Abbie. "But you have to admit he was a complete wanker. Is that what all the blokes on this site are like?"

"Not necessarily," said Joyce. "Mostly they are all horny as hell and some of them are quite fanciable. You've just had a bad start but don't let it put you off. Are there any other messages for you?"

"No," admitted Abbie. "Perhaps I'll give it another twenty-four hours. Shall we have a drink and forget about it for tonight?"

Chapter 5

Phil had been having a tiring day. He had been occupied the entire day carrying people to the vaccination centre on the outskirts of town in an old disused factory site. There were ample parking spaces for all the visitors who drove their own cars and some hastily erected tented areas where the vaccinations took place. There were numerous volunteers who directed traffic and the patients. Everything appeared to be organized on a military basis and each patient was taking between twenty to thirty minutes to be dealt with including a five-to-ten-minute post vaccination resting period. This latter time period was explained to each inmate as a few moments to allow each patient to recover from any dizzy or detrimental experience as a result of the vaccine when administered. When Phil spoke to one of the volunteers as he was waiting for one of his fares he was told that in all the experience of the volunteer who had worked there since it had been set up about three months before, no one had experienced a single dizzy spell. The man told him that he had seen literally thousands of people pass through the centre. He told Phil that it was better to be safe than sorry although Phil felt that each visit that he made to the centre took about fifteen minutes longer than it need have.

Most of his fares were elderly people who had no vehicle of their own. Each had different hopes or expectations of the procedure but one thing that Phil noticed was that the older each patient was, the more accepting they were of the whole procedure. The older they were, the more submissive they appeared to be. He found himself regarding all his fares rather as a shepherd or herdsman might regard his flock and he felt some guilt at having such thoughts. However, he still felt a sense of responsibility towards each of them regardless of how weak or fearless they may seem to be. He felt the need to help them each in a separate and individual way. He felt an alliance and sympathy for all of them although he realized that many of them were younger than he was.

Everyone who had been inside the tent for their vaccination appeared to be very satisfied. No one it seemed was disappointed with the procedure. Phil himself got jabbed while he was at the centre on one of his trips. He had to agree that the procedure was painless and trouble free. A few people he knew had complained of a sore arm after their vaccination, but no one seemed to suffer any serious effects.

All, that is except for one. The gentleman in question was of approximately the same age as himself, and Phil remembered him because he was wearing similar headgear to that which he himself wore occasionally, namely a woollen, knitted hat with a bobble on the top. It was not the same colour as Phil's hat but certainly made him think that it was probably made by the same manufacturer. He had never driven the man before and had only acquired him as a customer when he dropped off one of his regulars at the centre and was driving off on an errand when the gentleman hailed him in the outside car park area. Although Phil's car did not have a taxi sign on it, the gentleman must have seen him dropping off his fare so stepped forward and asked him if he would mind dropping him off back in town. Phil agreed and took him back to town and gave him a card with his telephone number upon it. When it was time for the man to have his second vaccination, he gave Phil a call and arranged to be picked up by him in the town centre and driven to the vaccination centre for his second dose. Phil collected him near the church just a block away from the town square. He recognized the man who was still wearing his woolly hat and his black backpack which he had worn the first day Phil carried him.

On this occasion the gentleman went into the vaccination tent but never came out. After what seemed to be an exceptionally long time Phil got out of his car and went to the entrance area of the tent. He vaguely recognized one of the volunteers stood outside the tent and engaged him in conversation. He explained that he had earlier delivered a passenger for vaccination but that he did not appear to have emerged from the tent. He described the gentleman as best he could and wondered if the volunteer had seen him. The other told Phil that the passenger he had described had indeed gone into the tent for his jab and had afterwards sat down for the customary ten-or fifteen-minute rest period but had then been found by one of the assistants unconscious in the chair. At first it was assumed that he had nodded off to sleep and so he had been left to his own devices for a while but then, upon closer examination they realized that he was not sleeping but unconscious. One of the doctors was called upon to examine him and an ambulance, which was already parked at the centre, was used to transport him to the nearest hospital Phil was disappointed to hear that and made his way back to town without a fare.

He returned just in time to collect Beryl Smithers from her house in time to deliver her to Tesco's. On route she informed him that she herself had an appointment for her first jab that day in about forty minutes time. Would Phil be able to take her to the vaccination centre straight from Tesco's? He confirmed that of course he could and then went on to tell her about the fare he had earlier delivered for a jab but who had then been found unconscious in a chair. That started Beryl worrying about the possible side effects of the vaccination process and the possible dangers to health. Phil assured her that one of the volunteers whom he vaguely knew and who had told him of the incident had also told him that it was the only single incident at the centre since it had opened and that apart from that one gentleman over fifteen thousand people had been vaccinated without mishap.

This seemed to re-assure Beryl and she asked about his children and told him about a program she had watched on TV the previous evening about operations in hospitals.

She told him that the program had advised that nationally many thousands of patients who were waiting for operations, were being placed on the backburner by the Health Service, and little or no operations were being carried out currently on patients suffering from cancer or problems such as she herself was suffering ie her hip that needed replacing.

"I was in such pain last night when I was watching the program," she said as they drove towards Tesco's. "It was as if the mention of the subject on the TV brought on the pain in a subliminal way. Not as though the pain is not always with me of course but as if it was made worse by the mention of it on the program," she said and began grunting with pain and shifting herself about in the passenger seat.

"No news yet about any date for your operation I suppose?" said Phil hopefully.

"No," she replied with certainty. "They made it totally clear to me that while this epidemic was going on there was absolutely no chance whatsoever of my operation taking place. And even if this Covid thing cleared up today there was a queue of unfulfilled operations before me which would take up at least a couple of years space. No, my only hope would be if I were able to go private, in which case I could have the operation in about a month. But there's no chance of that happening, it would cost me several thousand pounds which I do not have."

Phil expressed his sympathy as they drew into the Tesco car park, and he dropped her at the door and promised to wait there for her. When she returned with a trolley half full, he unloaded it into the boot of his car and then they set off for the vaccination centre where Beryl, with some pain and difficulty, got out of the car and made her way to the tented area for her vaccination. Phil parked nearby and waited for her. Through his windscreen he spotted the same volunteer that he had spoken to earlier in the day. As he had nothing else to do he got out of his car and walked over to him.

"Hello again," he said as he approached. "Any more news on that poor fellow who was taken to hospital earlier?"

The volunteer, whose name turned out to be Nick and had gone to the same school as Phil, shook his head.

"No, too soon I think though I must say he didn't look too good. The doctor who treated him did say however that it certainly wasn't anything to do with Covid."

"Oh," said Phil. "That's something I suppose, but I wonder what was wrong with him?" Nick shrugged his shoulders and said, "We won't know until the hospital have a good look at him, but the doctor thought it was probably a heart attack. Was he a friend of yours?"

"No," said Phil. "I didn't know him, I was just giving him a taxi ride." Just then Beryl emerged from the tent and staggered towards them grimacing and holding her hip with each painful step. Phil said goodbye to Nick and helped her towards his car.

Chapter 6

Stephanie and Percy Wilson were sitting in their comfortable home mentally twiddling their thumbs. Percy was trying to locate on the TV set a recording of a Rhyder Cup match which the European team had won and which he was certain had been correctly stored on the set, and she was crocheting a jacket for Rupert. She was knitting it in a pale -yellow wool, not because she considered that to be a suitable colour for her grandson but because she had sufficient wool left over from a previous project and she always hated to waste anything.

"Do you suppose Sheila will agree to Rupert coming round here tomorrow?" she asked.

Percy was still struggling with the TV controls and cursing under his breath because the set would not surrender up the golf match, he was so sure was in there.

"Er, I don't know, I'm sure. Oh, why won't this wretched thing let me watch the program I am trying to watch?"

"It's not as though she can argue that we are suffering from any complaint at the moment is it?"

"Hmm, what's that?" muttered Percy swearing quietly at the set which was not responding.

"I mean, neither of us has even the mildest cold or flu symptom have we, let alone the dreaded Covid. By the way, what exactly are the symptoms?"

"Hmm, symptoms?"

"What symptoms are those?" he asked still concentrating on the TV control.

"Oh for goodness sake!" she shouted. "You haven't been listening to a word I say have you?"

Percy stabbed his finger on the off control of the device he was holding and flung the thing down on the floor and stood up. "I don't bloody know," he shouted with such volume that his wife almost jumped out of her skin. "I'm going out into the shed," he announced with some vehemence and flounced out of the room and made his way into his garden shed where he had a chair made from cane with a cushioned seat. On a work bench he had a radio and he switched it on and sat quietly trying to organize or monitor his own thought processes. He tried to remember a time in his lifetime when his own existence had been so dull and futile, and he wondered what he was going to do next.

Life for him since the advent of the Covid epidemic had become almost intolerable. He could no longer see his friends and play golf with them. He had nowhere to go and nothing to do. He felt not as though he were at peace in his spacious home but a prisoner in a confined place where there was no interesting company, and nothing worked. He was uninspired by anything. He had taken to gambling on his smart phone and had already accumulated a sizeable debt which worried him greatly. He could not explain it to himself since he did not even enjoy gambling and only continued doing it in the hope that he could replenish the funds which he had already lost.

While he sat there with the radio broadcasting some classical music in the background, he took his smart phone out of his pocket and idly fingered the menu index and, almost without any real interest in what he was doing, located the gambling site which he generally frequented. He was immediately offered a plethora of gambling possibilities which ranged from football matches and horse racing events all over the world. Even though he was a sports fanatic generally, he still had no idea of the form of horses or football teams in for example Australia or South America. Despite his total lack of knowledge on the form book, he found himself placing a sizeable bet on a horse who was running in a race in Queensland in five minutes time at odds of twelve to one. A virtual outsider, he knew but the odds ensured that if the horse won the race, he would receive a hefty reward. It had happened before for him, so he knew that it was a possibility. He watched his phone as a recording of the race was shown on the screen. His chosen horse looked good for most of the race but on the final bend it was overtaken by another horse which stretched away in the final furlong.

Percy gave a sigh and then thumbed through the index and watched disinterestedly as a game of poker took place on the screen. He found himself deciding that cards or roulette just did not quite do it for him. Even though he was inexorably drawn into gambling he felt that the fact that he could still choose to bet on only sporting events gave him some hope that his problem was still capable of being cured. Subconsciously he became aware of the fact that his fingers had negotiated through all number of events on offer and finally left him to judge or decide upon a baseball game which was taking place in New York at the time he was watching. Despite having absolutely no knowledge or experience of either team, he found himself placing a bet on the result of the game. The radio gave forth an Oboe concerto in D minor by Tomaso Albinoni while he considered which team to back. Ten minutes later he discovered that the team he had wagered his money on had won the game, so in a matter of seconds his mood was lifted. His fingers then took him to an ice hockey match taking place in Canada.

Chapter 7

Abbigail was struggling with a case that had fallen on her desk. She could never bring herself to feel any empathy for someone whom she could not respect or admire. She appreciated that there was always a position for everyone and that every guilty man was entitled to have a spokesman. However, if there was no positive aspect which she could define and hold on to then she felt herself losing a grip of that which she should be holding fast and true.

The present file she held belonged to a security firm who had premises on an industrial estate on the outskirts of the town. Their case consisted of the loss or theft from their premises of a carton which contained a large amount of money in the form of bundles of fifty-pound notes shrink-wrapped in thin plastic sheets. The firm had been contacted by the deputy manager of the company who gave the details of the incident over a zoom contact interview which Abbie had already viewed.

The informant, Mr Jones the deputy manager was probably what gave her an uncomfortable feeling about the case. She was not completely sure why she felt that way about him. He was smartly dressed in a dark suit with a pale blue shirt and a darker blue tie. She noted that although he was probably no older than mid-thirties, he already had streaks of grey on the sides of his hair which was gelled and swept backwards away from his forehead. Strangely, Abbie thought, his eyebrows showed no trace of grey and were therefore surprisingly black compared to the hair on the top of his head. So too was the small pencil moustache below his nose which lent him, she thought, an appearance of the sort of character who always played the part of a trickster or cad in old black and white films which she had watched on TV when she was a child.

Mr Jones explained that the carton had disappeared from their depot the day before they had contacted them. As far as anyone knew, the carton, which was made of thin cardboard, had been in a particular storeroom at the depot. At the time of the supposed theft a couple of their staff were loading up a van which was secured in the firm's garage area at the rear of the premises. Both members of staff had been questioned and knew nothing about the missing carton.

Further, the inside of the garage area was fitted with a CCTV camera the tape or disc of the time the van loading, showed that what they had said was correct. The tape exonerated them by showing them loading up the van with the items for delivery and then climbing into the vehicle and operating the electrical doors to open to allow the van to exit

What the tape also showed was that after the driver and his mate got into the van another person appeared on screen from the inside of the premises and exited the garage on foot just as the van was pulling away. That person was not seen by the two operatives who were facing the other way, but he was recognized by Mr Jones as the cleaner at the depot, a man called Stephen Pike who had worked at the depot for about ten years and had been vetted when he was first employed and had never previously given any reason for the firm to mistrust him. The tape showed him to exit the garage area just in time to dip under the door which was descending after the van had exited. He was not carrying a carton but was wearing a black backpack. Although the tape did not reveal whether or not the back pack was full he did confirm that the backpack was large enough to contain the carton. Each bundle he explained contained one hundred notes making each bundle worth £5,000. The total number of bundles in the missing carton was fifty which meant that the total which had been lost or stolen was two hundred and fifty thousand pounds. Abbie gave a silent whistle in response to this information and asked if they had contacted the police. He confirmed that they had but so far, the police had not managed to find him.

"But since you have informed the police, what is it you are expecting us to do that the police cannot achieve?"

"Well," Mr Jones offered. "We did not want to leave the whole matter in the hands of the police. After all, they have had twenty-four hours now and achieved nothing. We need someone to do some research on our behalf and if and when he is located, we may wish to commence a court action against him. We need any investigations to be completely confidential and could not entrust them to a private detective firm."

Abbie advised him that her firm would of course be pleased to assist in any way but also told him that they would have to tread carefully otherwise they might end up being charged with interfering with police business. She asked him if the notes were all freshly printed and if so, did he have a note of the individual numbers and, if so, were they all consecutively numbered? Mr Jones confirmed that they were consecutively numbered and that he had transferred to her firm already a list of the numbers. He had also transferred a sheet of paper showing the name and address of the cleaner Stephen Pike. He suggested that Abbie contact him as soon as she had any information for him and to remember that in due course his firm would be reporting the matter to their Insurance Company and to be prepared to pass a copy of their file to the Insurance Company for their consideration

After her conversation with Mr Jones Abbie examined the contents of the file again and puzzled as to how she could solve this mystery or in any way do anything which the police could not achieve more expeditiously. She supposed that the first thing she should do was to call at Mr Pike's address but could not think that the police would not have already done this. She thought also that if Mr Pike really was the thief, that he would presumably have already beaten a hasty retreat. Did he own the property he lived in and if so, how was he planning, having made off with a small fortune, to gather the proceeds of the property which he had left behind him? She reasoned that such a plan would only be feasible if he had only rented his property. If he were an owner then by stealing the money he would only be making off with something worth approximately the value of the property he had left behind. That did not make any sense at all. If however he was a poverty-stricken man who only rented the property where he lived, a spontaneous theft of a carton harbouring a small fortune was more understandable.

Chapter 8

Phil was doing another run to the vaccination centre. This time his passenger was Oswald Swann who was waiting at the front of his building as Phil pulled up beside him. After a second or two had passed Phil realized that although he was parked right beside him Oswald had not seen him, or rather he had not recognized his car. Oswald continued to stand by the curb staring into the middle distance like a blind man.

Phil switched off his engine and opened his door and stepped out onto the pavement beside him.

"Morning Oswald," he said taking his arm to guide him. "Did you not recognize my car?"

Oswald did a double take and replied, "Oh I don't recognize any cars these days. They all look the same to me, I think they are all designed similarly, and all look the same. Not like the old days when they really knew how to design cars. Do you remember the old Jaguars?"

"I do indeed," replied Phil still holding his arm as he opened the passenger door for him. "Are your eyes still playing you up? How many fingers am I holding up?" he asked without even holding up a hand at all. Oswald looked towards him for a second or two and finally said.

"Two fingers, Phil." And settled himself into the passenger seat. Phil closed the door carefully and looked at him as he felt beside himself for the seat belt his eyes still fixed on the middle distance. Phil gave a grimace and said, "You really ought to take a visit to the Optometrist or the eye hospital you know."

"That ain't gonna happen, Phil. I've been into all that before and I can't afford it. I will manage, OK thanks."

Phil was not so sure or happy about that response. He thought if he had more time or a few bob to spend he would look into the matter of Oswald's eyesight. In the meantime, he set the car in gear and drove them both to the vaccination centre. He drew into the car parking area as close to the tented area as he could get. Oswald got out of the car and made his way to the tent and then disappeared inside. Phil sat in his car for a few minutes listening to the car radio until he noticed his old school chum who worked as a volunteer. He got out of his car and wandered across the carpark to talk with him.

They hailed each other and stood together in the carpark chatting. Phil asked him, "Did you hear any more about that guy who was here the other day, the one who was taken to hospital?"

"Yes, I did," said his companion. "Apparently, he died. The doctor who was here and who tried to treat him at the time normally works in the hospital, and he made enquiries and they told him. It seems he was right; it was a heart attack which he had suffered but he never re-gained consciousness. It was a great shame."

"Wow," said Phil in surprise. "That is a shock I must say. He looked fine when I dropped him off here. It just goes to show doesn't it, that you just can't take anything for granted can you?"

The volunteer shook his head. "No you certainly can't," he responded and then had to move away to help someone who had come for a vaccination and needed directions. Phil wandered back to his car still reflecting on how something unexpected like a heart attack can ambush anyone at any time. He also reflected that on such occasions there was probably always something that one had forgotten to do, and his mind took him back to the fact that he had always been intending to write a will but had never got round to it. He determined that he would bring the topic further up his list of priorities. He sat in his car for a further ten minutes and then spotted Oswald coming out of the tent and looking around. Phil could tell again that his fare could not see or recognize his car and so he had to get out and go and fetch him.

"All right Oswald?" he enquired as he approached him. Oswald squinted at him for a moment and clearly only recognized him by his voice.

"Yes, thanks," he said. "Nothing to it. That's my second jab, I think I must be just about immune to anything now," he chuckled as he said this. Phil took his arm and guided him back to the car and while they were walking, he told Oswald the news he had just heard from the volunteer.

"Would you believe that?" he asked. "Only the other day I was talking to him on this very spot and now he's gone. It makes you think doesn't it. Maybe you ought to think again about getting your eyes tested before it's too late, eh?"

Oswald shook his head emphatically and said, "I told you before, I've been into all that already and I cannot afford the cost of having an operation."

"But surely there must be some means of getting it done on the NHS?" he suggested.

Oswald shook his head again. "No definitely not," he confirmed. "In any event, even if there were some means of having it done for free there would be no space at the moment because there are too many people with Covid who are taking priority. No," he reiterated. "The only way is to have a private operation and I don't have the money to be able to afford that, and that is final."

Phil understood where he was coming from and wished that he himself were wealthy enough to help him. They both got back into the car and Phil drove him home. As he dropped him off at his basement flat, he watched as he made his way down the stone stairway to his cellar apartment and could tell that he was finding his way down by holding on to the hand-rail and by making exploratory footsteps before applying his weight to each step. As far as Phil could see he might as well have been walking in the dark.

Chapter 9

Abbigail was on her way to the college where she was studying a course on law. It was part of her employment contract that she worked in the office full time except for the day each week on which she attended the college. It was a term of her articles that she studied law for the five years of her articles period.

On her way to the college, she called at the address which Mr Jones had given her for the missing cleaner at the security firm. She knew that enquiries would have already been made but hoped that perhaps Mr Stephen Pike might still be in the house but had perhaps been temporarily sick or ill and therefore unable to get to work. A generous ringing of the doorbell produced no response from inside and so she decided to make enquiries nearby.

She started with the property next door. The house where Mr Pike lived was a cottage in a cul-de-sac which contained four such properties in all. The first neighbouring house produced no response and so she determined to return at a different time of the day, presuming that perhaps the neighbour was at work. There was a similar result on the other side. This brought her to the final cottage which was at one end of the cul-de-sac. The doorbell was answered by a very elderly and deaf lady who appeared to suffer partially from Alzheimer's' disease. She was completely unable to assist but suggested Abbie returned in the evening when her son would be there and able to tell her about Mr Pike.

Abbigail decided to return at a different time of the day hoping perhaps in the early evening, that someone would be available to give some information. She continued on her way to the college which was in a town which was about ten miles down the road. The class was shared by about twenty others who were there for different reasons. Most of the class were in their final year at the college and were studying law at an A level basis. There were also two or three retired people who were studying simply for an interest in life. One other member of the class was in a similar position as Abbie. She was an articled clerk in a firm in the town where the college was situated. Her name was Mavis Davies, and she was newly married and about the same age as Abbie. Because they were in the same predicament they were thrown together and became friends. They always sat together in the classroom and usually spent the lunchtime break together chatting about the subject they were both studying. They had not been in a classroom for very long without becoming good friends.

Today they went to a nearby coffee shop during the lunch break. They both had a sandwich and a coffee and settled down for a chat. Abbie began to tell her about the matter she was concerned with in her firm namely the matter she had just dealt with on the internet with Mr Jones the gentleman from the security firm and their missing cleaner and the missing money. She told her that she had called at the property on her way to the college in the hope that she would be able to find him and sort out the problem but that she had been unsuccessful.

"Even if he was there and I found him, I do not know for certain that he took the money," she told Mavis.

"But why not simply leave it to the police to sort it all out?" suggested Mavis.

"That's what I said," responded Abbie. "But Mr Jones said that in the first place they did not trust the police to do a really efficient job. Also, they said they needed someone to fight their corner for them rather than being merely impartial. And further, if the missing man turned out to be guilty of taking the money, they need us to commence legal proceedings against him. The police won't do that whatever the outcome of their enquiries."

Mavis nodded understandingly and said, "What you need is a private investigator who would be working entirely for you. Someone who would be able to apply all his time to the job and who is not diverted by other jobs which might take precedence over your matter. I know just the man. He has a history in the CID and has done work for the firm I work for; in fact, he has an office in the floor above us. His name is Charlie Chivers and he's brilliant I have used him and been with him when he's working, and I can assure you that he is the best." She dug into her handbag and rummaged about and finally came out with a card which contained Charlie's details. She handed it to Abbie and urged her to give him a ring.

Abbie examined the card which read, 'International Detective '(Charlie Chivers) and then gave the address which was the same as the address of the firm of solicitors at which Mavis worked, 'Huw Roberts & Co'

"So," enquired Abbie. "International detective eh, what exactly does that mean?"

Mavis shrugged and said, "I'm not really sure, I'm also not sure that he himself knows what it means. I suppose it means in theory that he is prepared to go anywhere in the world to solve a mystery. Having said that, I do not know of any projects which he has undertaken outside the UK. I guess the title is something he invented to try to convince people of how flexible and experienced he is."

"So, an advertising stunt?" suggested Abbie.

"Eh well," responded Mavis. "More perhaps a way of suggesting his preparedness to go anywhere required. But don't be fooled by it, he is very down to earth and efficient and completely confidential. And he also has very useful contacts in the local CID."

Abbie placed the detective's card in her purse and promised Mavis that she would consider it and thanked her for the recommendation. She also promised to report back to her as to her progress on the case. They spent the rest of their lunch hour chatting with each other about things other than the law. Mavis told her that she was a newly-wed who had been an articled clerk with Huw Roberts & Co for the best part of a year and was thoroughly enjoying the experience. She told her that she had recently married

George Davies whom she had met whilst working in the Civil Service. She said that the office they worked in had been closed and so each of them had to move to a different part of the country or leave the department they worked in. She herself had chosen the law as a career having been encouraged to do so by a lady barrister she had met, and her husband had inherited a large amount of money from his grandmother and no longer needed to work for a living.

"When you say, 'a large amount of money' how much do you mean?" asked Abbie.

"Oh, several millions," replied Mavis modestly.

"Oh wow!" exclaimed Abbie. "That is fantastic, how lucky are you?"

"I know," said Mavis apologetically. "It was a shock for George. He had no idea that his grandmother was well off. He lived with her because his parents were killed in a car accident when he was young."

"So, he is an orphan millionaire?" Mavis agreed that that was the case.

"How lucky are you?" she remarked.

"But it's not how it sounds," Mavis assured her. "I knew him long before he got his inheritance. We had already decided to get married before his grandmother died."

"Well," said Abbie with some envy. "I did not mean to imply that you were a gold digger, I was just saying how envious I am that you managed to find a husband who is a millionaire. I cannot even find myself a boyfriend let alone a husband. Almost no dates are possible during these

Covid times. I joined a dating site recently but could not find anyone interesting so far."

"Oh really," said Mavis with interest. "I have never been on one of those sites. Aren't they a bit dangerous? I mean, you never know who you are talking to do you?"

"Well, that's what I said to my friend Joyce who introduced me to it, but she assured me that such sites are completely safe and secure."

"Oh yes," observed Mavis sceptically. "But how can they be completely secure?"

"Well," explained Abbie. "Joyce tells me as long as neither party meets up or reveals any details, one is always totally safe."

"But isn't the whole object of going on the site to meet up with a guy?" asked Mavis with a puzzled look.

"I know," said Abbie. "That's exactly what I said." They both looked at each other and burst out laughing.

Chapter 10

Stephanie and Percy were having one of those days which could only be described as extremely annoying. It was annoying for Stephanie primarily because her daughter-in-law, Sheila had, once more, denied her access to her grandson Rupert. She had been told by her daughter-in-law that due to the prevalence of positive tests in their local area she was keeping Rupert at home for a while and not allowing him to mix with anyone including his grandparents. She assured her that as soon as the general climate improved, they would all be coming round to see them. Her coup de grace which she delivered over the telephone was that much of her concern was on behalf of Rupert's grandparents themselves. She emphasized how easy it was for toddlers to pick up the Covid strain and whilst being unaffected themselves pass it on to older people e.g. Stephanie and Percy, who were much more vulnerable.

For Percy, the day was annoying due to the fact that his wife was upset about not seeing her grandson again.

"I honestly can't see why Rupert can't come round to see us," she told him. "After all, it's not as though we have been mixing with anyone is it? Neither of us have been out for weeks, we have been getting our groceries delivered by van and everyone we have seen within the last three months approximately has been tested with negative result. How is it possible for us to have the disease or pass it on to Rupert?"

Percy nodded in agreement and muttered, "Absolutely, a lot of fuss and bother about nothing. I was thinking of having a go at sprucing up that spare bedroom. I thought I would pop down to the DIY store to get some paint and sandpaper. Do you fancy a trip?"

"Well yes, it would make a pleasant change to go anywhere I must admit, but do you think it would be a good idea? I mean, what would Sheila say if she found out we had been there? That would give her more ammunition for refusing us access to Rupert would it not?"

"Well, I'll tell you what, why don't we simply not tell her?" he suggested. "Come on get your coat, I'll back the car out and Sheila won't need to worry about us will she?"

Against her better nature Stephanie agreed and they got in the car and drove to the local B&Q store where they spent some time wandering up and down the aisles viewing paints and wallpapers. Percy eventually selected some paint and wallpaper and pushed their trolley towards the checkout area.

"Hello Percy," said a voice from behind. "Doing some home improvements then?"

Percy turned to find that the voice belonged to one of his chums from the Golf Club. He gave a wry grin and indicating the trolley said, "Hello Sid, yes, I've decided to do up our spare bedroom. At least it gives me something to do when I can't play golf eh? What have you been doing with yourself?"

"Oh, not much," responded Sid. "I haven't been able to do much for a few days. I came down with a cough and a cold so at the insistence of my wife I got myself tested and they said I had Covid. So, I have not been able to go out for a few days. But I felt OK, no symptoms really."

Stephanie said, "But are you safe to be out and about after just a few days, I thought you had to isolate for at least ten days otherwise you could be spreading it all about."

Sid gave a suave smirk and said, "I know, but quite honestly I think it's all a load of bollocks really. I don't know for certain if it was anything other than a cough or cold and I always felt OK."

Stephanie was appalled at the cavalier attitude of her husband's friend and dragged Percy away by his arm scowling at Sid as they went to the checkout area. When they had paid for their goods and climbed back into their car, she unleashed herself upon her husband just as he was expecting.

"I can't believe what I just heard," she said. "No wonder the disease is spreading globally when there are morons like that about."

"Oh, don't be too harsh on him," urged Percy. "You heard what he said, he didn't feel any symptoms."

"No symptoms!" she repeated with incredulity. "He admitted he had a cough and cold type symptoms and furthermore that he was actually tested and told that he had it and then in a couple of days he is out and about wandering around in a DIY store. I really don't know what Sheila would make of it if she were here."

"Well," he said irritably. "I suggest that you do not tell her about what has happened. We'll get one of those do it yourself test kits and test ourselves and if we are negative then no one needs to know do they?"

Stephanie gave a grimace that seemed to indicate that she would not be able to keep this topic to herself. Percy was almost certain that she could not and therefore was putting all his hopes on a negative test. He could not believe what a plonker his chum Sid had been.

Chapter 11

Phil awoke early in the morning and made himself some bacon and eggs for breakfast with some coffee. He went outside to check his vehicle. There was a frost this morning which had left some ice on the windscreen and windows. He took his scraper out of the shelf inside the driver's door panel and began scraping off the frost on all the windows. He examined the overall condition of the vehicle and decided that today he would take it to the car wash and have a good look at the inside of the car and perhaps give it a vacuum clean. He always liked to keep the car in tidy order so that his passengers were not dissatisfied with it.

He had awoken early this day because he had been booked to take someone to the airport early in the day. A seven thirty morning plane meant that he would have to get his passenger to the airport by at least six thirty. The flight in question was not an international one; there were few of them in the period of epidemic. The aeroplane that Phil had to arrive for was one bound for Edinburgh and his passenger was a businesswoman who implied, when booking her journey, that there might be further journeys booked if this one was satisfactory. Phil did not mind early morning trips and indeed almost never did any evening work.

His fare lived about five miles away and so got cracking in plenty of time and was outside the lady's house about ten minutes before she had booked. He did not mind and was quite happy to sit outside her house with the engine ticking over so that by the time she emerged the car was warm and cosy. Bristol airport was about a twenty-minute drive and at that time of the day the traffic was very light. When they arrived at the departures area of the airport the lady must have been fully satisfied with Phil because she informed him that she was returning in two days' time and asked if he were able to meet her at the airport and gave him the time of her intended arrival. Phil told her that he would indeed be able to meet her and wished her a safe flight. On his journey home he wondered what taxi firm she had used before, (on route she had informed him that her journey was routine), and what they had done to prompt her to change her allegiance. Whatever it had been, he reflected that their loss had been his gain.

On his way home Phil was passing the entrance to a car wash establishment so he was reminded that his car needed a good wash, so he drove into the place and had a wax wash. For ten pounds he got the outside of his car power sprayed by an eastern European gentleman who wore wellington boots. After this his car was pulled through the automatic part of the car wash machine and sprayed with wax and then water and being sponged and automatically beaten with giant rags hanging from the roof. Finally, his car was subjected to a blast of hot air which dried it off and eventually he emerged from the machine and was able to drive home in a bright shiny vehicle.

He drove home where he had just enough time to enjoy a cup of coffee before his second fare of the day who was Beryl Smithers who, as usual, wanted a lift to Tesco to gather some supplies for the week. After he had finished his coffee, he left the house to make the journey to Beryl's house. As he approached his vehicle, he was surprised to notice how shiny and new it looked and he made a mental note, when he had the time to spare, to vacuum out the inside of his car and give the interior a polish.

Having reflected on that he then got into his car and drove to the house of Beryl Smithers and rang the doorbell. It seemed to be an age before Beryl finally answered the doorbell and he could see that she was having more trouble with her hip. She was walking this morning with the aid of a walking stick which Phil had not seen her use before. She came to the door carrying her shopping bag and grimacing with every step. Phil could see how painful it was for her and offered his arm and helped her towards the car.

"What you could do with would be one of those invalid trollies," he said.

"Hah," she replied. "That's another thing I can't afford."

With some difficulty Phil managed to get her into the passenger seat and made sure she was buckled into her seat belt. He then went round to the driver's side of the vehicle and strapped himself in, checking his rear-view mirror before driving away.

"Seriously though Beryl you have to do something. You are obviously in a great deal of pain and need that operation. There must be some source for the money, have you tried everything?"

"Yeah," she said wearily. "There is only two alternatives, get it done for free on the NHS (which is likely to take years now that every hospital bed has a Covid patient in it), or go private and pay for it. I could have it done by the end of the month if I could pay them three thousand quid which I haven't got. No, all I can do is keep buying pain killers, Phil."

When they arrived at Tesco he parked outside the door and fetched a small trolly for her. This was a help for her because it not only allowed her to put her shopping inside it but also acted like an invalid frame which she was able to lean upon. She was clearly unable to do her shopping without the trolly and Phil watched sympathetically as she disappeared into the store. When she eventually returned, he assisted her back into the vehicle. She flopped into the passenger seat with a great sigh, leaving Phil to unload her shopping into the boot of his car and return the trolly to the trolly park. Then he drove her home and the same procedure was repeated at her house. When all that had been achieved Phil seated himself in her kitchen while she made him a cup of coffee. He did not really need or want a coffee, but Beryl always liked to provide one, so he accepted with good grace. He watched as she slowly and painfully made her way around the kitchen area grimacing with pain and holding on to table and work top with every painful step.

"If I had any cash to spare, I would gladly pay for your operation, Beryl," he assured her.

"I know you would Phil, and that is very kind of you to say so, but I know very well that I am going to have to wait a lot longer for any relief from my pain. That is, unless you buy a lottery ticket, and you get lucky, eh?" she chuckled at her own humour.

"Well," replied Phil optimistically. "As it happens, I do buy a lottery ticket each month and I can promise you here and now that if my ticket comes up, I will pay for your operation, Beryl."

"Aw, that's very sweet of you," she said, rummaging into her purse. "In the meantime here is your taxi fare."

Phil finished his cup of coffee and said his goodbyes and drove home. He parked his car outside close enough for him to reach from the electric point inside. With a long electrical extension lead he was able to bring his vacuum cleaner outside and clean the inside of his car which he had been promising himself he would do for days. First, he took out the foot mats and gave them each a beating and a hoovering, and then he started on the floor of the vehicle beginning at the front area first. His first task was with the driver's side which was the dirtiest because it was the most used. The passenger side at the front was not so lucky because not many of his passengers sat in the front passenger seat. Once the front area had been cleaned, he decided to push the front seats as far forward as he could in order to have the room to get the vacuum cleaner in the rear of the vehicle. The driver's seat refused to move when he tried to push it and he discovered that something was jammed underneath it. He struggled to remove it but finally discovered that it was a backpack which he brought out into the daylight. He could not think who this bag belonged to and tried to remember which fare had carried it. Eventually he recalled that it was the man whom he had delivered to the vaccination centre, the man who, according to the doctor on duty, had later died in hospital. He looked inside the bag to see what was there and to see if there was any information as to who the man was.

A cursory examination of the front and side panels of the bag showed them to be completely empty. When he looked inside the main area of the bag, he found that it too was empty except for a large brown paper package which he unloaded and unwrapped. He was astonished to find that the carton contained smaller several smaller packages each about the size of a mobile phone, which, at first he thought were packs of playing cards, and then immediately realized were fifty-pound bank notes. He scratched his chin and began to wonder what to do with this discovery.

Chapter 12

Abbie got up early and was having some cereal with a glass of orange juice when her father came into the kitchen.

"Morning, Dad," she said through a mouthful of muesli. "What will you be doing today?"

Percy stood beside her for a few minutes gazing out into the garden as if he were miles away.

"Humm," he said, in a faraway voice. "What did you ask my love?"

"I said," Abbie repeated more slowly and deliberately. "What will you be doing today?"

Her father turned to her and kissed her on the top of her head and said, in a lacklustre way, "Oh, I don't know, probably, I'll get on with sprucing up the spare bedroom."

Abbie consumed her final spoonful of cereal and looked at him.

"But why are you doing that? There is really nothing wrong with the room as it is at the moment and it's not as though we are expecting any visitors, is it?"

Percy considered this carefully and said, "Well, your mother decided that now, during the pandemic, would be an appropriate time to freshen it up a bit. Also, it gives me something to do doesn't it. I cannot play golf or visit the pub, can I?"

Abbie nodded and took her bowl to the sink and swilled it off and placed it on the drying rack. She turned to face him and said, "Well, I must be off to work, I've got a busy day today." She gave him a quick hug and told him she loved him and left the kitchen to gather her coat from the hallway and shouted a cheery goodbye and left via the front door which she slammed behind her.

Percy remained in the middle of the kitchen gazing out into the garden. His wife marched into the kitchen.

"Was that Abbie going out? I wanted to ask her something before she went."

"Hmm?" mumbled Percy without looking round. Stephanie looked at him and repeated.

"I said I was meaning to ask her something before she left," she said then, seeing the faraway look in his eyes she said more sternly, "Oh, never mind."

Abbie arrived at work early and began reviewing the files which were on her desk. There were a varied number of topics which the files covered, and she was grateful for that. There were several which dealt with conveyancing matters, and some which involved matrimonial or divorce problems and several other files each covering different subject matters. Mr Morris who was the senior partner of the firm always tried to share the files meticulously among those beneath him and felt a particular responsibility towards Abbie, who was the firm's only articled clerk at the time, in order to give her as much experience as possible.

The file that attracted her attention the most at the present time was the case of the loss or theft of the carton full of bank notes from the local security firm. She was aware of what Mr Jones the deputy manager of the firm had told her, but she was desperately bewildered as to what she should be doing with the case. She did not wish to go back to Mr Jones for more instructions or explanations but did not know how to proceed. She felt that her only course of action was to discuss the case with Mr Morris and see what he had to say. She realized that this made it look as though she was young, indecisive and unsure, but she had to admit to herself that that was entirely the case. She knew that if she went ahead without asking for advice and something went wrong then it would look much worse for her.

She went along the corridor and knocked on the door of Mr Morris' office. He called 'Come in' and so she opened the door and entered his room. It was a much larger room than hers and had a large bookcase against one wall full of law books. He also had a large bay window with a view of the High Street, and a big leather Chesterfield couch against the other wall and two smaller cane chairs before his desk for visitors. Abbey seated herself on one of these and opened the file in front of her and gave him all the information about it and confessed that she was flummoxed as to what action to take. She told him what Mr Jones had told her and explained that she had been to the address of the suspected thief but that her visit had been unsuccessful. She admitted that she felt out of her depth trying to carry out private investigations partly because she had no experience of such activities and because she was conscious that any sleuthing she might do could result in complaints or criticisms from the local police who presumably would be carrying out their own investigations. She told him she had been highly recommended to use a private detective known to the girl who was in the law class at college with her, but she was reluctant to instruct him because the instructions given by Mr Jones was that any enquiries had to be carried out with the utmost confidentiality. She showed him the card of Charlie Chivers the International Detective which Mavis had given to her and asked him what she should do.

Mr Morris looked carefully at the card and considered the information she had given him. He was himself a vastly experienced solicitor who had been appearing in the local Magistrates court and the nearby County court for many years. He nodded and said, "Yes, I am familiar with this gentleman who for years was a member of the local CID. He is a very experienced information gatherer and entirely trustworthy. I have used him myself on several occasions and found him to be exemplary. You would be hard pressed to find a better private detective. Mr Jones' instructions for confidentiality would not preclude employing this gentleman to make enquiries on your behalf. You must not be confused and /or misled by those instructions into thinking that it is your job to carry out those enquiries. It is not, it is your job to make the right decisions and do the best job for the client. Any mistakes this man makes whilst he is employed by us would be covered by our own Insurance. However, I do not believe he will make any mistakes and so I suggest you contact him and give him instructions to locate the missing man."

Abbie knew as soon as Mr Morris had confirmed what she had to do, that that was exactly what she had wanted to do. She just had not had the courage or the experience to make the decision. She told her boss this and thanked him for his advice. He assured her that she had made the right decision in bringing the matter to him and he congratulated her on that. She thanked him again and went back to her own room.

She sat at her desk and looked at the card and after a second or two she rang the number.

"Chivers Detective Agency," barked a voice into her ear which almost made Abbey jump out of her skin. She stated her name and her business and told him she had been recommended to contact him by Mavis who worked at Huw Roberts & Co.

"Yes, I know Mavis very well," he confirmed. "She works downstairs from me, where exactly are you?"

Abbie told him and he said, "That's not very far, I'm going that way this afternoon. I could call in and see you on my way and pick up your instructions if you like?"

Abbie said that would be fine and a time was arranged for two-thirty p.m. that afternoon. She said she looked forward to seeing him. As soon as she put the phone down, she started to type the instructions which he would soon be collecting. She told herself that she had made a significant step forward.

A couple of hours later, Charlie Chivers entered the reception area of Featherstones solicitors and was soon shown into Abbie's office room. She saw him as a late middle-aged man who was overweight and dressed in a grubby elderly gaberdine coat. His saving grace for her were his friendly brown eyes which, despite his age appeared to glint like those of a child.

What Charlie saw was a young attractive girl with blond shoulder length hair and an easy-going nature. It did not surprise him to know that she and Mavis were friendly. He told her that his office was in rooms above the offices of Huw Roberts & Co solicitors where Mavis worked.

"She is an exceptional young lady," he said as he scanned the instructions which Abbie had presented him with. "She will eventually become a first-class solicitor. I note from this instruction report that you have a similar style to her. If you turn out to be half as good as her you can be proud of yourself."

"Well," said Abbie. "Those are very kind words. I hope you won't mind me repeating them to Mavis when I next see her?"

"Not at all," said Charlie gathering up his coat and his instructions. "I am very fond of Mavis and think that you will be able to learn a lot from her. I will report back as soon as possible."

With that he walked out of her room with a jaunty pace and a cheerful wink.

Chapter 13

Abbie felt some confidence in what Charlie had said and the manner of his approach. She felt a great relief to have off-loaded the matter temporarily. She looked forward to meeting up with Mavis at the college the following week. Having passed the ball over to Charlie she felt an injection of energy towards her remaining files and got on with the rest of her working day. When she left the office, she felt positive and satisfied with the way her day had gone. As she walked home, she thought about her internet dating adventure which, so far, had been remarkably unsuccessful. She took her phone out of her handbag and gave her friend Joyce a ring.

"Hi," she said. "How's it going with you? Are you free to come to my place this evening for a drink and a chat? Perhaps we could have another go at that dating site? Maybe you could help me find a decent man who might be worth spending some time with."

Joyce agreed that she would be glad to come to her house and would call round at about seven-thirty p.m.

When she got home, she found her mother in the kitchen making pies of some description. Stephanie always chose to make several pies at the same time so that some of them could be frozen immediately leaving one to be eaten on the same day.

"So," she said. "What's on the menu tonight? Where's Dad?"

"Pork pie with meat and veg, ready in thirty minutes. He's in his shed again. He's been there all afternoon; I just don't know what he finds to do in there all the time."

Percy was sitting in his cushioned chair gazing at his phone. He had been watching a basketball game which was taking place in Israel. Although he did not know anything about the teams who played in that country, he had always considered himself to be a good judge of sporting teams anywhere and having watched the game for five minutes he convinced himself that the team wearing white were superior in almost every way. Every single one of their players seemed to be taller than the players wearing red. In basketball, he knew that height was always a tremendous advantage. He also noted that the players in white appeared more muscular and robust and so he judged that over the length of the game their height and strength would see them through. He wagered a large amount of money on the white team and settled down to watch the game.

His initial belief that the team in white would gradually pull ahead of their opponents proved to be incorrect. As the game wore on the red team showed themselves to be faster and more skilful and he watched with a feeling of despondent understanding that the red team were going to win with ease. He raised his hand despairingly to his forehead and wondered how much he had lost this week. He knew it was a considerable amount, indeed he could not remember the last time he had won on any sporting event. He ground his teeth relentlessly and knew that he had to try to retrieve some of his losses with a bet that might save his bacon. If he could do that he promised himself to cease gambling for ever.

The door of his shed creaked as it opened, and Abbie stepped inside.

"Hi, Dad," she said and put an arm around him as she leaned in to give him a peck on the cheek. "How are you doing?" she said affectionately. "What are you doing out here, why don't you stay in the house with mum?"

"Hello sweetheart," he said looking up at her as a single tear rolled down his cheek.

"Ooh dear," said his startled daughter stroking his shoulder. "What is the matter, what is it?"

Percy shook his head quickly and said, "I was just reminiscing, and it brought a tear to my eye. It's nothing darling, nothing at all."

Abbie gave him a big hug and said, "Aww come on, no more sitting out in this cold old shed in the cold. You're coming back into the house with me and mum. She has made a lovely pork pie and it will be ready in a moment." She gathered him up and led him back into the kitchen. Once inside they each sat on a kitchen stool and watched Stephanie finishing off the cooking. She was stirring the gravy and checking the roast potatoes and the pie.

"About another five minutes," she estimated. "Why don't you open a bottle of wine, darling," she said to Percy who duly got up and chose a bottle from the rack behind the kitchen door. He opened the bottle and took three glasses out of the kitchen cupboard and poured the glasses and handed them to his wife and daughter and then took his glass back to his stool.

"So sweetheart, tell us, what sort of day did you have?"

Abbie swilled her glass around momentarily and said,

"Oh, I met an International detective today."

"Wow," said her mum. "And what on earth is one of them when it is at home?"

Abbie went on to describe for them her meeting with Charlie Chivers who would, she hoped, soon be solving a case she was working on. She was always keen to tell them about her work and she knew that they were both extremely proud of her. At the same time, she was always careful not to tell them too many details about her work which she knew was confidential. Her mother was serving up their meals onto plates on the work island in their kitchen. They decided to eat where they were and not to bother eating around the table in the dining room. As they ate together Stephanie asked her more questions about her work. When the meal was finished Abbie announced that her friend Joyce would be coming round shortly so she would go up to her bedroom. Soon after she had said this the doorbell rang and Abbie rushed to answer it and showed Joyce up to her bedroom.

Abbie got a drink for them both and switched on her lap-top and waited for it to warm up and connect her to the dating site. As soon as things were joined up they both found that she had two visitors this evening. The first one was called Lawrence and gave his address as Penzance in Cornwall. Abbie winced when she saw his address which was over one hundred miles from where she lived. She was not prepared to carry on any form of romantic association with anyone, however good looking, who lived that far away. When she read his profile description, she was even more certain that he was not the man for her. He declared that he was into what he described as moderate violence; his profile picture showed him sitting next to some chains and hand cuffs and a large whip. The man looked older to Abbie than her own father and as they gazed at the screen Abbie put her finger down her throat and gagged. Joyce too was unimpressed and could only manage a reasonable judgement.

"Well, at least he's completely honest," she said but nodded as Abbie's finger hovered over the delete button. She pressed the button, and he was gone.

The next candidate was more promising. The first thing that interested Abbie was the fact that he hailed from Bristol. She was comforted with the knowledge that if they ever got close enough to meet it would not take long to physically meet. The man described himself as 'Pete the plumber'. The profile described him as being thirty-one years old but to Abbie he looked at least ten years older than that.

"Hmm," she said to Joyce. "What do you think of that?"

Joyce carefully read the description and nodded appreciatively while doing so. She pointed to one sentence in the paragraph which indicated that he lived in a thatched cottage and ran his own business. The downside of the description was that he fell into the category of being divorced and having three children. She thought when she read that information that if he really were only thirty-one years old, he must have started his marital career at a very young age. That reinforced her original impression that he was at least ten years older than he had declared. The opening message told her that Pete found her to be very sexy and wanted to take her for a ride in his boat.

"Wow," said Joyce enthusiastically. "A boat, eh? Let's hope it's a bit bigger than a rowing boat. You have to message him back; he sounds almost too good to be true."

Abbie agreed and so between them they composed a reply which Abbie entered onto her laptop but before pressing the 'send' button she paused to read the message and allow Joyce to approve it. The message read, 'Hello Pete, how are you today? Good to hear from you. I'm thrilled to hear that you have a boat. How big is it? Where do you keep it? I would love to go for a ride on it. Is it big, or wide enough, to allow me to lie topless on the deck? Would you like to spread suntan lotion on my back?'

Joyce approved the message and agreed that it was provocative enough without being too lewd and offered sufficient seductiveness without seeming course or vulgar.

She agreed that Pete the plumber would not be able to resist this message. She nodded in agreement as Abbie pressed the 'send' button. They both took a sip of their drinks and spent a further half hour reviewing all the male entries on the site to see if there were any suitable candidates for Abbie to approach. She decided that none of the entries interested her enough to tempt her into sending a message.

Chapter 14

Charlie Chivers the international detective had returned to his office after collecting the instructions from Abbie. Seated in his garret room above the offices of Huw Roberts & Co solicitors he skimmed through the papers she had given him concerning lost or stolen package from the security firm. He thought to himself that the matter looked quite straight forward. He looked up at the picture of the calendar girl on the wall of his room which overlooked his desk. She was young and busty and, to Charlie, so appealing that he had not been able to bring himself to replace the calendar when the year had ended. Her picture had been on his wall now for two years. He reflected that it would have to be a superb picture on any new calendar which he chose to replace the photograph of the bare breasted young lady on the present one.

    He gathered up his papers and his raincoat and with one final admiring glance at the calendar girl's breasts, left the room to go and find out the whereabouts of the missing cleaner. His old but reliable Ford Motor vehicle was parked nearby. He opened the door, seated himself behind the wheel, checked one more time the information as to the cleaner's address, and started the car and set off.

When he reached the house that Abbie had earlier visited, he parked outside and got out and looked at the small cul-de-sac which contained only four cottages which looked like ex council owned, partially run-down properties. He told himself that even if the man himself was not in his cottage, the occupiers of the other three properties were bound to have information as to his whereabouts. He rang the doorbell and waited and in a few moments the door was opened by a woman who looked young enough to be described as still in her thirties.

"Eh, Mrs Pike?" he said with a raise of the eyebrows.

"No," she replied tearfully. "He was not married, I am his sister. I came round earlier to see him but the police called to see me and informed me that he had died." She wiped a tear from her eye and said, "It's been such a shock for me, and I have a lot to do sorting all his stuff out, what can I do for you?"

Charlie had always been a quick thinker and had the advantage of being an ex-CID officer. "I appreciate that you have had some sad news, I presume it was our uniformed branch who called round to give you the information?"

She nodded and continued to weep quietly, "I just wasn't expecting it, I don't really know where to start."

Charlie nodded sympathetically and said, "I understand how you must feel. In all my years in the CID I have had my share of times when I have had to have conversations like this. Would you mind if I came inside to talk with you for a while?"

She summoned him in with a wave of her arm and led him into the lounge which looked very small and basic. There was very little furniture in the room and only a small threadbare rug on which there sat a tired looking two-seater sofa and an armchair which did not even match it. Clearly, Stephen Pike had not been a rich man. He seated himself on the sofa and extracted a note-book from the papers he was carrying. He knew that a notebook was something all members of the public expected to see officers using.

"So, just to refresh my mind, what did the uniform branch tell you?" he asked.

She seemed slightly surprised and said, "Didn't they tell you?"

Charlie coughed apologetically, "No, I have been engaged on another task and came straight here without going back to base. Perhaps you would not mind letting me know exactly what they told you?"

"Of course," she said. "Well I was here anyway, I usually call round every week and do some housework for him. Without me doing that regularly for him, this place would look even worse than it does. Ironic really isn't it when you think that his job at the security firm is cleaning. Perhaps when he had finished his work there, he was always too tired of cleaning to do anything here," she said almost apologetically and then by way of explanation she said. "Stephen has always had learning difficulties. He always struggled at school and obtained no academic qualifications. He was I think, lucky to get the cleaning job with the security firm and was not able to ever manage to handle any job more complicated. He never had much self-confidence and was happy doing a job which he could manage. I have always helped him wherever I can, and I know he needed support and guidance."

Charlie was nodding as he made notes and asked, "How long had he been working there?"

"Oh, more than ten years I would guess. It was the first and only job he had managed to find. He loved working there and was so proud to have a job. There was a time after he left school, when he could not find work and his life was without any organisation. For a while we were all concerned that he might fall in with a bad lot of companions. He could not form friendships or keep those he had made, and his life was unstructured. The job made all the difference to his life and made him feel worthwhile. We were all so happy for him but always knew that he needed our support. We certainly never had any idea that there was anything wrong with his heart."

Charlie continued nodding his head and made some more notes in his book. "So, they told you it was a heart attack that caused his death, is that right?"

"Yes, that's right," she said. "He was due to go for his second Covid vaccination that day. I remember distinctly because I had to make the arrangements for him. He was not able to manage anything like that by himself, so I know that was where he should have been that day. As it happened, he ended up in the local hospital and I don't know if he ever had his jab or whether he had the attack before his vaccination appointment time which I remember was ten-thirty a.m."

"So," said Charlie. "Just to be sure, what exactly did the uniformed branch tell you about how he suffered his attack and where he was at the time?"

"They told me that he had arrived at the hospital in an ambulance which had been called to the vaccination centre but nobody knew who he was. He was unconscious when he arrived and although they tried to revive him, he never recovered. They only discovered who he was when they found his library card in his pocket. Ironically, although he was virtually illiterate, he loved books and particularly those with pictures in them. He could never afford to buy books but would always borrow some each week to look at the pictures therein. He always had a few books inside the backpack which he wore and usually it would be books on the subject of fishing which he was really interested in. He loved those books, particularly the books which had pictures of the various fishes and /or the places to catch them. He spent most of his spare time either by the beach or on the bank of a river."

Charlie took more notes and asked, "How did he get to the vaccination centre do you know? Did he have a car?"

His sister shook her head. "No," she said. "He couldn't afford a car. He must have caught a bus or a taxi or scrounged a lift from someone."

"Do you have a photograph of him which I could borrow," Charlie asked. "It might make it easier for possible witnesses to identify him when we ask questions about him."

She confirmed that she could provide one and left the room to find it. She soon returned with a good photograph which she handed him. Charlie studied the picture of a young man smiling and proudly holding a fish for the camera. He asked her how old the picture was. She replied that she took the photograph last year.

"Oh, good," said Charlie. "So, quite up to date."

"Yes," she confirmed. "It is a clear likeness."

"Well," said Charlie. "That's very helpful of you. Could I please take a few more details of you for future reference, your full name and address and perhaps a telephone number if you have one?"

She said her name was Jennifer Pike (she was unmarried), and gave him her phone number. She lived not far from her brother's cottage. Charlie thanked her again for her help and handed her a card and urged her to contact him if she thought of anything else which could be of assistance. She examined the card carefully and said,

"So, you are a private detective, is that right, I thought you said you were with the CID?"

"No," said Charlie. "I used to be and I still help them in a lot of their investigations, I am hoping that I can help you in this matter. Did the uniformed branch give you all the details of their likely enquiries and concerns?"

"No," she said. "What concerns?"

Charlie explained that a package had gone missing from the security firm which contained some money, and the police might well be interested to know if her brother had any knowledge of it. Jennifer was astonished and asked.

"Do you mean that they might think he stole it? That is just not possible," she said. "I told you he had learning difficulties, he was a complete innocent. He would never knowingly steal anything; he was not capable of dishonesty."

"Hmm," said Charlie thoughtfully. "Hang on to that thought and do not let anyone persuade you to think otherwise."

"I will not," Jennifer assured him. "I just know he would not have stolen anything."

Charlie gathered up his notes and thanked her again and took his leave. He made his way back to town but on his way called in at the vaccination centre in the hope that he could pick up any information. He parked in the car park area and observed the situation and the procedures. He saw the members of the public, presumably the daily influx of patients, who all walked from their cars, each wearing a mask, and entering the tented area where he presumed the vaccinations took place. Outside the tent there were a few helpers standing about and directing anyone who seemed unsure as to where to go.

Charlie got out of his car and put on his mask and wandered over towards the tent There was a male helper about the same age as himself who was standing outside the entrance of the tent. He spoke to the man in a friendly manner, "Hello, I wonder if you could give me some help."

The helper pointed towards the tent, "Go straight in there and give your details. What time is your appointment date?"

"Well as it happens, I don't have one for today but I do have an appointment for tomorrow morning. I just came today to have a look and find out what the procedure is."

"So, will that be your first jab or second?" asked the man. "Or are you here for a booster, I guess not if you don't know the procedure?"

"That's right," lied Charlie. "It will be my first."

The man nodded, and pointed again to the tent. "You just go in there and give them your details and they check their lists etc and then direct you on through to the main tent where they do the jabs. Afterwards they advise everyone to take a seat and rest for about ten minutes before getting back into their cars to drive home."

Charlie nodded and said, "Oh, so is there any chance of any adverse effects after one has had a jab?"

"No not generally," said the man. "But of course it is always better to be safe than sorry."

"Yes, I understand that," said Charlie. "But all the publicity about vaccinations on the TV and radio etc assure us that there is no possibility of anyone suffering any ill effects from the jab. Isn't that right?"

The man nodded. "Absolutely," he responded. "No ill effects whatsoever, at least none at this centre."

"But," said Charlie. "There is a minority of public opinion that advocate that vaccination is bad for you, and furthermore, a friend of mine was out here the other day and told me that he saw a chap being taken away to hospital in an ambulance following his having a jab?"

"Ah," said the man. "The anti-vax people just don't know what they are talking about and have no plausible evidence to support their claims. Also, that man who your friend saw being taken away in an ambulance had suffered a heart attack so his condition had nothing to do with the Covid jab."

"But how can you be sure of that?" asked Charlie sceptically. "After all if he was adversely affected by the jab, they would try to keep it quiet so as not to scare the public surely?"

The man shook his head emphatically. "No, absolutely not, the doctor who examined him when he was here works at the hospital and he went back there at the end of the day and enquired about him and was assured by his colleagues there that the man had suffered a heart attack. He was sitting here in the after-vaccination rest area when he simply appeared to go to sleep in the chair. There was no violent reaction to the vaccination."

"But that must have been difficult for him. When he recovers presumably, he will have to return to collect his car?"

"No," said the man. "He will definitely not be returning, unfortunately he died in hospital. In any case, he did not arrive here in a car, he came in a taxi. I remember seeing him myself and I also remember talking to the taxi driver, I went to school with him. I can see him now; he came to ask me where he was because he thought it had been a long time."

"Wow, I'll bet," said Charlie. "So, if you went to school with him no doubt you can remember his name or the taxi firm name?"

"Um, let me think," said the man. "Johnson was his name but I am not certain about his first name, it was either Bill or Phil, I'm not certain but I do know he doesn't drive for a taxi firm, he is an independent. He drives a black Ford, why do you ask anyway?"

"Oh, no reason really," said Charlie. "It's just that I won't have my car tomorrow so I was thinking of getting a taxi instead. So, Phil or Bill Johnson you say, no doubt he will have a telephone number in the book?"

The helper nodded and then had to go to assist someone. Charlie walked back to his car and drove back to his office to consider matters. When he got back to his office, he tried to locate the telephone number of Phil nor Bill Johnson but was unable to locate one. Instead, he telephoned the number of the biggest taxi firm in town and asked if Phil or Bill worked for them or, if not, did they know him. The lady he spoke to said that Mr Phil Johnson was known to them but that he drove independently and was semi-retired and only worked part time. She said they had a note of his phone number and after a couple of minutes she was able to give it to Charlie who thanked her. He dialled the number she had just given to him, but the phone kept ringing and ringing. It did not divert him to a recorded message. He made a mental note to try again later.

Chapter 15

The next day, Phil was up bright and early. His first fare of the day was Beryl who always went to the local Tesco branch on the same day every week. He arrived at her door and got out of his car and gave her doorbell a ring. It seemed like an eternity before she opened the door and said good morning to him. She was wincing with pain and almost unable to walk and moved to the car very gingerly. She finally collapsed on the front passenger seat and as she was adjusting her seatbelt Phil asked her about the pain she was suffering.

"You really ought to do something about that hip of yours," he said. "Surely the hospital can do something to alleviate the pain you are suffering?"

"No, Phil," she said, buckling herself up. "There are no vacant beds at the moment. They are all full up with Covid casualties. It has been that way for about two years now. The NHS can give me a new hip but there is no way they can do it for at least the next two or three years. The only way of getting one would be to have it done privately and that, I have been told, would cost me around ten to twelve thousand pounds and I sure don't have that kind of money. So, I will have to carry on taking the pain killers and stay on the sofa with my feet up watching TV."

"That can't be right," responded Phil. "When you are in so much pain, there must be some way of accelerating the system. After all, you paid your tax and National Insurance all your working life, didn't you? Surely, three years is too long to keep you suffering."

"You are right, Phil," she said. "But going private and paying the money is the only way. Believe me. I have looked into it and there is no other way."

Phil shook his head and started the car and drove round to Tesco's where he parked as close to the door as possible. He left her in the car for a second or two while he went and selected a shopping trolley for her and brought it round to her side of the car. With difficulty she got out of the car and then leaned heavily on the handles of the trolley and treating it like a Zimmer frame, she limped into the store to do her weekly shop.

After about thirty minutes she emerged again, and Phil took the trolley from her and helped her into the passenger seat and then unloaded her shopping into the boot of his car. He then took the trolley back to its parking area and returned to the car and sat down in the driving seat.

"It's so distressing to watch you struggling as you do Beryl. Is there no grant or charitable gift system available to you to be able to get to the head of the queue?"

"No chance, Phil," she said. "What I need is a *Prince Charming* with oodles of money and nothing else to do with it."

She snorted with laughter.

"But that is not going to happen. Home, James."

Phil put the car in gear and drove her home. There he helped her into the house and then unloaded all her shopping from the boot of the car. When he was inside the kitchen, he stored all her food items into her fridge and various cupboards as directed by her. She then made a cup of tea for him and they sat down at her kitchen table together for a while. Phil asked her.

"So how long, after paying the money, would you have to wait for your hip operation, Beryl?"

"Oh, no more than a week or so. They told me that they could do the operation at the drop of a hat. But that is not going to happen Phil, like I said, I just don't have access to that sort of money, and I don't have any savings."

Phil gave some thought to her problem while he was gathering his coat and preparing to leave.

"Well, don't give up hope Beryl," he said as he left. "Your *Prince Charming* might come along one day."

"Yeah," she replied. "And pigs might fly."

Chapter 16

The international detective sat in his office gazing wistfully at the picture of the calendar girl on the wall. He picked up his telephone and dialled the number which the taxi firm had given him. Once again, the phone call went unanswered.

Charlie decided to make another call. He dialled the number of the DCI at the local police station. This man had been a colleague of Charlie when he had worked in the CID. When he had first met him he went by the name of Des Onions. About twenty years later when he had achieved a number of promotions, he was known as Chief Detective Inspector O'Nighons. The DCI answered his phone and heard Charlie's voice.

"Des, it's me," he said. "How are you fixed for a lunchtime drink at the Jubilee Inn?"

"Definitely," said Des. "I was about to give you a ring to suggest the same thing. I'll see you there in about fifteen minutes."

Charlie was the first to arrive which was normal. His office was close to the Jubilee Inn whereas the police station where Des was based was a good fifteen minutes' walk away. He entered a neat and tidy bar room which was never crowded at lunch time. Standing behind the bar was the licensee Reg Partridge, a small red-faced corpulent gentleman with a bald head. As usual he was drying and wiping glasses with a tea towel.

"Morning, Charlie," he said cheerfully, reaching immediately for a pint glass without Charlie asking for anything. "How are you today?"

Charlie said that he was good and while waiting for the glass to be filled, he surveyed the wall behind the bar which was full of photographs of many different well-known personalities all of which had one thing in common; all the celebrities were photographed standing next to a smiling Reg Partridge.

"Will Des be joining you today or are you drinking alone today?" he asked reaching for another glass. Charlie confirmed that Des was on his way, so Reg started to draw a second pint. Charlie perused the lunchtime menu and retired to a nearby table and began reading his Daily Mail. After about ten minutes the door opened, and Des walked in with a cheery good day to Reg who returned his greeting. He scanned the lunch menu and chose an item therefrom and called across to Charlie for his choice which was steak pie and chips. He also agreed to have another pint which Des ordered and paid for. He then took his own and Charlie's replacement pint over to the table and greeted his friend.

"So, how's your work going today?" he asked Charlie who responded that he was doing quite well and asked him if he was busy.

"Yes, quite busy," replied Des. "Got an interesting case the other day."

"Oh yes," said Charlie. "And would that be the loss of money from the security firm?"

Des looked genuinely surprised and said to him, "How on earth did you hear about that? there has not been any press release on that so how have you heard about it?"

Charlie then told him about the instructions he had received from the solicitors Featherstones, "A young lady called Abbigail who, guess what, only goes to law lessons at the college with Mavis who recommended her to instruct me to make some enquiries into the loss or theft of the money. Her firm have been instructed by the management to make enquiries and try to trace the whereabouts of the money discreetly and quietly."

"But why would they wish to involve a firm of solicitors in tracing the money when the police are already involved and using our own resources to trace the money?"

"Aah," sighed Charlie. "Good question. I guess they don't have that much confidence in you to get to the bottom of it. Also, if a suspect is located then it follows that some legal action may be required. Further, almost inevitably an insurance company will be in the picture and probably picking up the bill. I guess they wanted to be involved in all the investigations rather than being beholden to you."

"So, what have you discovered so far?" asked Des.

"Well, I don't know how much you know already. I'm not sure if your uniform branch is in touch with you or whether you are all joined up yet. The guy that the firm presumably fancy as being the thief is the cleaner at the premises but had gone missing, but it seems he went to the vaccination centre and then had a heart attack and died on the way to hospital. The uniform branch must have had his name and address from the centre and have already been to his house to report his death to his sister, but I don't know if they were ever aware of the incident at the security firm. In any event, I went there and saw her and what she told me convinced me that he probably did not steal the money. He was a simple character with learning difficulties who was not capable of any dishonesty."

Des took the details from Charlie and said he would check details with the uniform branch and come back to him again to compare notes.

"What I would recommend is that you make a few enquiries about the deputy manager of the security firm. He is the man who instructed the solicitors, Featherstones, on the internet. This young lady, Abbigail whom I spoke to had an instinct about him. She told me he looked slimy and untrustworthy, and I looked at their internet conversation and have to say that I agree with her. He looks dodgy to me. Check his history I would suggest, and I will see what I can find out about him also."

They both parted company promising to work together to track down the precise movements of the cleaner Stephen Pike following his exit from the security firm premises as seen on CCTV carrying a backpack, and his arrival at the hospital.

Chapter 17

Phil had a busy day. It was the last day of the week for him even though it was only Wednesday. His day started with a fare with Oswald Swann. He left his house after giving the inside of his car a quick sweep and polish. He parked outside Oswald's place and gazed up at the Victorian façade of the building in which he lived. He found the grandeur of the building quite overwhelming. Several of the properties in this magnificent edifice, particularly the ones at the front with the large bow windows, were owned by well-off people. The only occupant in the building who was not well-off was the person who occupied the damp dingy cellar area below the stairway to the main front door, namely Oswald Swann.

When Phil turned up the man himself was stood at the foot of the front doorsteps smoking a matchstick thin home rolled cigarette. As Phil opened the door of his car and stood in front of the property, he was greeted by his fare asthmatically coughing and croaking and desperately trying to clear his throat. He greeted Phil with a wheezy 'good morning' and then announced that he needed to gather some things together before being ready to leave. He made his way to the few steps down to his basement flat and nearly tripped and fell and just managed to clutch the hand rail and save himself the fall. Phil winced as he watched the vulnerability of his fare.

Oswald emerged in five minutes clutching a plastic bag which contained a few items including a pair of gloves and a scarf. He opened the passenger side door and seated himself beside Phil who said, "You nearly went a cropper going down those steps earlier. It was a close shave. Your eyesight is getting worse isn't it. Are you sure that you can't get any treatment for your cataracts?"

Oswald breathed in deeply and said, "I've told you before Phil, it is a straightforward operation which I cannot get on the National Health system. If I could afford to pay for it I could have it done next week, but it is several thousand pounds which I just don't have so I have to put up with things."

Until you lose your footing and fall down those steps and break your neck thought Phil, as he turned the key in the dashboard and put the car in gear and they set off on the journey.

When they arrived, Oswald stumbled into the doorway of the business he was visiting, and Phil waited in the car for him to return. While he was waiting Phil reflected on the situation of his fares Oswald and Beryl whose lives could be vastly improved by the expenditure of relatively modest sums of money. He had in mind of course the cash he had found in his car, presumably left behind by the man he had taken to the vaccination centre. The man who had suddenly had a heart attack and died.

He had a dichotomy of thoughts in relation to the backpack which had been left in the car. He had never been anything other than an honest man. He had never committed any crime or misdemeanour in his life but admitted to himself that he was tempted to use some or all the cash for good purposes. He knew that his duty was to hand the money in to the authorities and that to retain it was, in effect stealing by finding. On the other hand, he argued to himself, so long as he spent the money on good causes and not solely on himself, it was somehow all right. Yet, he knew all along that any judge in a court of law would take a different view.

Again, on the other hand he reflected that the money was all new and unused and freshly printed and therefore belonged not to any individuals but to a large impersonal organisation such as a bank or an insurance company. It would be no doubt insured and its loss would not cause any hardship to anyone. He knew that this was a spurious argument, but he also felt that he was seduced by it. What assisted him in thinking in that direction was something that had happened to him about two years ago. He had then been diagnosed with prostate cancer which was too extreme for him to be cured and it had already begun to spread to other parts of his body. He knew that if he used the money for the purpose he had in mind, and if he was found out and even if he received a prison sentence, he would spend very little time in gaol.

On the subject of committing the crime and the detection of that procedure he wondered about the ways in which his involvement could be traced. He was vaguely aware that numbered bank notes could be traced by police but he had no idea how that system worked. He supposed that the tracing procedures were always bound to be retrospective. That is, that police would know into which bank notes were paid and that CCTV camera shots could be viewed and meticulous piecing together of actions taken could eventually lead to the thief. But, he thought, what if for example a note was passed to someone remote where there were no CCTV cameras. The only evidence would be the identification by the trader or whoever who had been given the note. If, he thought for example, he purchased a hot dog from a burger van parked on an empty road and he was wearing a disguise, how on earth could the burger salesman remember him or identify him?

He thought carefully of an example of somewhere in which he could try out his theory. His requirements were that he should find a business which had no CCTV cameras either inside or outside their business premises. He had one in mind, a small shop in a back street in town, which sold locks and keys and other ironmongery. In addition, he was aware that there was a small café on the other side of the road which afforded a view of the lock and key shop. He thought he could take one note out of the carton and use it to purchase an item from the shop and thereafter watch the premises to see if any police called to make enquiries.

By the time Oswald re-appeared he had decided to carry out his plan to test the detective powers of the police.

He took Oswald home and then went on to finish the rest of his duties for the day, always planning to withdraw one of the notes and to visit the ironmongery shop the following day.

Chapter 18

Stephanie and Percy were at home in their kitchen diner area soon after breakfast. She had just put the phone down having had a conversation with her daughter-in-law Sheila. She reached for the kettle and asked her husband if he wanted a cup of coffee. He said he did, and she switched on the kettle and got the cups ready.

"That was Sheila on the phone," she said. "She has to take their car in for an MOT so she will be round in a minute to drop off Rupert with us while she goes to the garage."

Percy's eyebrows raised and his face brightened up as he acknowledged this information.

"I'll get the box of toys out for him. Also, I'll get that old train set out of the attic and set up the track in the spare bedroom. He likes the train."

"But I thought you were going to decorate that room. You can't leave that train set permanently spread out all over that floor. You can't decorate around it. Last time you got it out it stayed there for weeks."

"Well," he responded. "In the first place it wasn't my idea to re-decorate the bedroom, it was yours, and in the second place, it is only a five-or ten-minute job to pack up the bits of track and pop them back in the attic. I only left it out before because Rupert was coming round every day before the Covid epidemic."

"Yes, well," said Stephanie frostily. "As soon as Covid struck she stopped him from coming round, but of course when it suits her, he can come round. Perhaps we should count our blessings I suppose."

"Well," said Percy diplomatically. "She's only doing what's best for her child I suppose."

"Oh, for goodness' sake Percy, why do you always take her side? She does what suits her not Rupert. If it didn't suit her to bring him round today, because the car needs fixing, she would not be coming. She did not bring him round last week did she, why was that do you suppose? Because the car didn't need an MOT that's why."

She handed him his cup of coffee and said.

"It's about time you realized what's going on and stop kowtowing to everything she does."

"That's unfair," he protested. "I am just trying to see both sides."

"Well," she asserted. "It's about time you showed a bit more backbone and stood up for me sometimes."

Percy rolled his eyes and picked up his cup of coffee and began to leave the kitchen.

"I'm going in the shed," he muttered as he left the room.

"Hmph," declared Stephanie to the closing door. "That's right go off to your man cave!"

She busied herself in the kitchen cleaning and clearing the surfaces and packing away the dishes and plates that had been drying on the draining board. As she stacked the plates away she heard a car arrive outside and immediately thereafter the sound of a car door slamming. The doorbell rang and she hurried to the front door and opened it to find her grandchild Rupert stood on the door mat.

"Hello, Nanny," he said with a big smile on his face. Stephanie knelt down and hugged him to her and, looking over his shoulder could see Sheila unlocking the boot of her car and taking out a plastic bag full of items for her grandchild. She came to the front door and kissed Stephanie and then they all went through to the kitchen together.

"Where is granddad," demanded the child looking disappointed.

"It's all right darling," Stephanie assured him. "Granddad is out in his shed," she indicated. Rupert cheered up immediately and straight away ran towards the outside door and rushed out to the shed where he found his grand dad and grasped his hand and led him back into the kitchen area. His mother and grandmother were already seated at the kitchen table while the kettle was already boiling for a cup of tea.

Stephanie made cups of tea for the three adults and an orange juice drink for Rupert who was already playing on the floor with Percy who was plucking various toys from the box which he had previously brought out of a cupboard. The two of them spent the next twenty minutes playing happily on the floor while the two women chatted to each other.

"I should not be too long at the garage," said Sheila, I just have to drop it off and collect it in about one hour. I will spend the time in between doing some shopping and then come back to pick up Rupert. She then stood up and reached for her coat and leant down to give her son a hug and a kiss.

"Now then," she exhorted sternly. "You promise me that you will be a good boy for Nanny and Granddad while I'm out." She gave him a kiss and made her own way out of the front door.

Percy gave his grandson a smile and said, "Shall we go upstairs and play with the train?"

Rupert whooped for joy and jumped up and went upstairs with Percy laughing and chattering all the way. Stephanie spent some time tidying up the kitchen once more and washing up the teacups and saucers. She then followed the two children upstairs and sat down on the bed to watch them playing with the train set. They both clearly enjoyed themselves for about thirty minutes until Rupert finally announced that he wanted to go back downstairs. They all rose and went back downstairs where Rupert immediately resumed his enjoyment of the toy box. After about twenty minutes Stephanie produced from the fridge a freshly-made sponge cake with fresh strawberries and cream which Rupert demolished with relish.

No sooner had he finished a second helping when his mother returned. She announced with some frustration that the car had failed the MOT test on a couple of minor points which the garage had agreed to put right the following day at ten o'clock in the morning if she brought it back which she had agreed to do.

"So, if I bring Rupert round just before ten o'clock will you be able to look after him?" she asked. Stephanie confirmed that that would be all right and that Rupert was welcome any day. Sheila coughed that point away and collected his items and told him to say goodbye to Nanny and Granddad, and they all walked to the front door. Rupert embraced them both then followed his mum to the car. Sheila locked him in the back seat and waved them both goodbye and drove away.

Chapter 19

Phil was enjoying one of his days off. He did not always have the same days off each week. He was flexible about it and if he had lots of journeys booked (usually by telephone), he would work. If he had few or none he would generally decide to stay at home. He always found things to do and was never bored with his own company.

He drove his car into town and did a bit of food shopping. He then decided to visit the ironmongery, lock and key shop. He had remembered to bring with him one of the crisp new fifty-pound notes from the package he had stored at home. He walked down the side street just to do a quick reconnoitre and to rehearse his steps in his mind. He had remembered that he had decided to wear a disguise so took out of his pocket a Covid face mask which he clipped behind his ears. He also produced a pair of sunglasses which he donned. Before entering the shop, he looked into the window, partly to decide what he would wish to buy and partly to look at the reflexion of himself in the shop window glass. Although he was close to the window, he failed to recognise himself and was satisfied to note this. He spotted in the window a locking device for his up and over garage door which was offered for just under fifty pounds.

He walked into the shop and heard a bell ring inside the shop as he opened the door. He could not see any sign of a CTV camera system anywhere. At the sound of the bell a thin middle-aged man with a bald head and thin wire glasses emerged from a backroom.

"Good morning," he said cheerfully. "How can I help you?"

Phil looked around broadly as if he did not know what he wanted. Finally, he indicated the item in the window which he had already decided to purchase. The man nodded and went out into the back room and returned with a newly boxed version of the item he had selected. Phil handed over the fifty-pound note, and the shopkeeper hardly glanced at it as he deposited it in his cash register and then passed the item and the receipt to Phil and said thank you.

Phil turned and walked out of the shop slowly, pretending to glance at a few items on display in a modest attempt to add an atmosphere of casual indifference to his visit. When he finally exited the premises, he strolled across the road and entered the café and ordered a cup of milky coffee and seated himself in the window to get a good view of the shop across the road. He opened his newspaper and having read the sports pages, he attempted to complete the crossword puzzle. After about one hour and having finished his second cup of coffee he realized two things.

Firstly, he noticed that all the time he had been there no one went into or came out of the ironmongery shop across the road. Secondly, he realized something which he wondered why he had not thought of it before. It was the police procedure for tracing numbers on banknotes. It occurred to him that the police would only be notified of the spending of listed banknotes by local banks who presumably be given lists by the police themselves. This procedure, he appreciated, would take at least twenty-four hours, possibly longer, before the police would be notified.

He mentally cajoled himself for behaving as naively as he had done. If the police were ever going to call at the lock and key shop following notification of the note being passed across his counter, it would not be for at least two or three days. He realized that he was wasting his time sitting in this café expecting something to happen and almost laughed at himself for not thinking the process through in the first place.

He folded up his paper and returned his cup and saucer to the counter on his way out of the café. He made his way back to where he had parked his car, several streets away, and then drove home to consider what he had done and how he could monitor the procedure further. On reflection he supposed that a further visit to the café was superfluous. He also thought that whatever the processes of recovery the forces of law and order could employ, they certainly did not have the means of detecting his use of the banknotes in time to prevent the operations he was planning for Beryl and Oswald. He knew, almost certainly that by the time he was discovered he would be so close to death that the possibility of any gaol sentence was virtually meaningless.

He reflected on the circumstances of Both Beryl, Oswald, and countless others who had worked hard all their lives and paid taxes and National Insurance but due to the situation which the Covid pandemic had imposed upon the system generally, they were unable to receive the care and attention which the National Health system had promised or guaranteed for them since its inception in the past under the oversight of Nigh Beavan. This was, Phil thought, Covid Injustice.

Chapter 20

Abbie awoke early and showered and dressed herself and went downstairs for some breakfast. In the kitchen, she found her father already dressed and sitting on a kitchen stool nursing a cup of coffee and staring vacantly out of the window.

"Morning, Dad," she said brightly. "You're up early today. What are you doing this morning?"

Percy remained otherwise engrossed.

"Hmm?" he said distractedly.

"What are you thinking about Dad?" she asked, selecting a bowl and a box of cereal from a cupboard and then opening the fridge to get some milk.

He turned his gaze back from the window and said to his daughter, "Hello darling, I was miles away. Just thinking over one or two things." He still had a vacant look on his face.

Abbie spooned a mouthful of cereal down her throat and asked him.

"What things have you been thinking about, eh?" she asked.

Her father gave a crooked smile and resumed his examination of the view out of the window.

"Ooh," he said reflectively. "Perhaps the futility of everything.

Abbie turned her head with surprise and said, "Awe, Dad, why so melancholy? What's up?" She came round the table and gave him a hug and he mumbled into the hair on the top of her head, "Oh, I'm OK, sweetheart. You get off to work and don't worry about me."

They were interrupted by the entrance of Stephanie who came into the kitchen wearing her dressing gown. She reached for the kettle and filled it with water and plugged it in.

Abbie pulled herself together and reached for her coat which was hanging over a stool. She scooped up her handbag which was on the stool and wished her mum and dad goodbye and left to go to work. Stephanie took the cup of tea that she had just made, back up to the bedroom with her. She had a shower and got dressed and after about forty minutes she took her empty teacup downstairs.

She found that the kitchen was empty, and she assumed that her husband had retired to his shed. She got on with her housework and spent about an hour or so hoovering and polishing. She took a break and put the kettle on for a cup of tea. She made a cup for herself and one for her husband and took his cup out to the shed. When she entered the shed, she was surprised to find that he was not there. She took the cup of tea back into the kitchen. She wondered where he was; she went upstairs to check the spare bedroom, but he was not there either. She assumed that he must have gone out to get some more supplies for the decoration of the spare bedroom. She thought, rather irritably that he might have had the decency to let her know he was going out. She hoped he had remembered that his grandson was coming round later in the day and that he would be back before that time arrived.

She got on with some more housework and then made another sponge cake which she knew would delight Rupert. After another hour she heard the doorbell ring and assumed it was Percy who had perhaps gone out without his door key. She went to the door ready to tell Percy off but found instead her grandson standing on the mat. She gave him a hug and a kiss and the child went straight on into the house while his grandmother stayed on the doorstep waiting to greet her daughter-in-law. Sheila unloaded Rupert's coat and a bag of toys from the back of her car and climbed the steps to the front door and gave Stephanie a kiss.

Rupert re-appeared from the inside of the house and asked his grandmother, "Where's granddad?"

"Oh dear," said Stephanie gently giving him a cuddle. "He had to go out darling but I hope he will be back in a minute."

"Where has he gone?" enquired Sheila.

"I don't know," responded Stephanie, I just went upstairs for a few minutes and when I came back he was gone. I presume that he must have gone out to get something for the re-decoration of our spare bedroom. I hope he will have the decency to return before Rupert goes home."

Sheila then decided that it was time to go and informed Stephanie that the garage had told her that the work they had to do to her car would take them about thirty minutes.

"So," she said, I should be back within the hour. "Now be a good boy for Nanny," she told him and gave him a kiss.

Stephanie and Rupert then settled down on the floor to play with his toys, and before too long they had nearly exhausted all the toys in the bag he brought with him. She found the box of toys which they kept in their house for him and that re-energized Rupert. In what seemed to be in no time at all, the doorbell rang again and they both went to answer it and found mummy back on the doorstep. Stephanie insisted that before they went home, they should each partake of some freshly made sponge cake. Rupert said, "Goodie." And clapped his hands together. They went bac k to the kitchen and Stephanie made another pot of tea for Sheila and herself and found some orange juice for Rupert, and then served each of them some slices of sponge cake. When Rupert had eaten two slices his mother announced that it was time for them to go home and she packed up the bag which she had brought with her and picked up the child's coat.

"Well," she said. "Give Percy our love and tell him we are sorry to have missed him."

"Yes," replied Stephanie. "I'll give him a piece of my mind when he finally gets back."

Chapter 21

Charlie Smithers the international detective was sitting in his office sipping a cup of coffee and gazing at the picture of the calendar girl on the wall in front of him. He looked longingly at her bare breasts and made a kissing gesture. He shook himself together and applied his mind to the details he had received from Abbie a few days ago. Her internet search of the security company and its staff had revealed that Mr Jones had joined the firm about ten years ago and had come to them from a position in the security department of a large import export firm in London.

He reached for his little black book where he kept a note of all the telephone numbers of contacts he had ever made. His volume was in a muddle, and he cursed each time he referred to the book because it was not arranged in alphabetical order. As always, he made a mental note to re-arrange the contents of the book in order to make any future searches a lot easier.

Eventually, he found the number he was looking for. It was an old colleague who he had served in the police force with. The man had transferred to the Metropolitan police force some years ago but kept in touch with Charlie from time to time. He answered Charlie's call immediately and after a brief friendly chat about health and families

Charlie told him why he had phoned, and his colleague promised to do some research and get back to him.

The man phoned him back in about fifteen minutes and was able to tell him that his checks on Mr Jones had revealed that he had worked in London only for a year or so. Prior to that he had worked in Hong Kong in the security department of HSBC bank. He also confirmed that there was a rumour that in Hong Kong there had been some jiggery-pokery which his contact was unable to check up on since the takeover of the island by the Chinese state. Charlie thanked him for his help and then immediately telephoned Des and told him what he had discovered about Jones.

"So," he said. "My hunch about this guy Jones was correct, but since the Chinese took over Hong Kong so I have no contacts which would enable me to find out anything else about him."

"Well," said Des with surety. "I certainly know someone who I believe might be able to help. I'll give him a ring and see what he can find out and see you in the Jubilee Inn as usual at lunchtime."

"Right, Ho," said Charlie and then hung up.

A few minutes later he dialled the number of Abbie's firm and spoke to her for a while. He told her what he had discovered about Mr Jones and wondered if there had been any progress on her side. She told him that there had been no further progress at her end but thanked him for the update. She was pleased and excited to know that Charlie had such influential contacts and looked forward to hearing from him further when he had seen Des.

When Charlie had said goodbye Abbey had paused a moment, before getting back to her work, to consider the behaviour of her father that morning. She wondered about the wistful look in his eye and the chance remarks he had made to her in the kitchen while her mother was still upstairs. She made a note to herself to spare some more time to be with her father; she thought perhaps this evening she would suggest to him that she and he could do something together such as going for a walk together or go to the cinema together or perhaps just do a puzzle at home together.

Chapter 22

After her grandson and his mother had left Stephanie busied herself around the house doing some laundry and some ironing. She always listened to the radio while she was ironing. She found it a therapeutic experience, and although she would never say she positively enjoyed it, she nevertheless endured it with some contentment. The radio helped her to maintain a satisfied tolerance of the pastime. She had been struggling with several sheets and pillowcases when she heard the sound of a car door slamming and shortly afterwards, she heard the doorbell ring. She assumed that Percy had finally come home and had gone out without carrying his own door key. With some slight annoyance she went to answer the door and was quite surprised to see a police car parked upon the forecourt and a male and female police officers stood on the doorstep.

"Hello, Mrs Wilson, is it?" asked the male officer awkwardly.

Stephanie nodded, already feeling nervous. "Has there been an accident?" she asked.

"Er, not exactly," said the male officer. "Can you please confirm that your husband drives a Mercedes car with registration number eh (he consulted his notebook and read out the number), colour grey?"

Stephanie was immediately now scared. "So," she said with alarm. "There has been an accident, how is he? Where is he?"

The man coughed confidentially and said, "Do you mind if we come inside to talk with you for a while?"

Stephanie ushered them inside and they all went into the kitchen diner. She offered them a seat and also sat down. Once more, the man did the talking and he said, "I am very sorry to tell you that your husband was found today in his car which was parked in the wasteland on the outskirts of the wooded area on the hillside. It was a dog walker who discovered him in his car and telephoned us. I am sorry to say he was dead."

Stephanie covered her nose with both hands and burst out crying and said, "But what happened? Was it a heart attack?"

"I'm afraid not, ma'am," he replied and coughed again. "Actually, there was a pipe attached to the exhaust pipe and the engine was running. It appears that he committed suicide."

Once again Stephanie cried out in horror and cried even more. The female officer rose and went to her and put her arms around her. Stephanie was shell shocked.

"I can't believe it," she wailed. "Why on earth would he wish or need to do that?"

"Well," said the male officer. "We have not completed our investigations yet. We have your husband's telephone which we will take a look at but in the meantime, we are wondering if you could give us any clue as to why he might have done this. I can confirm that he left no note of explanation. Is there anyone who can be with you at this difficult moment? PC Spencer here can stay with you as long as it is necessary."

Stephanie sobbed pitiably and managed to say, "My daughter will be home from work shortly."

They continued to console her, and the female officer made a cup of tea for Stephanie and as she was sipping it the door opened and Abbie walked in. She was already nervous because she had seen the police car parked outside, but additionally, finding her mother in tears, she feared the worst. While her mother continued to weep, the male officer explained the whole situation for her and presented her with a card with his details thereon.

Abbie was as shocked as her mother had been but felt somehow that she should try to maintain some calm in order to support her mother. Eventually the two police officers felt able to leave the two ladies together but promised that they would keep in touch and advise them of any developments. After they went Abbie telephoned her boss Mr Morris and explain what had happened. The following day was a Friday and he straightway told her to take that day off work which would then be followed by the weekend. He told her to take as much time as necessary, but Abbie felt that her mother's sister who lived nearby, would probably come round to stay temporarily to support her mother, and in which case she (Abbie) might come into work on the Monday. Mr Morris told her not to worry, but if she felt able to come into work on the Monday then he would be pleased to see her.

The following day Stephanie spent most of the day on the telephone talking to friends and relatives Each call took an age and was often interrupted by bouts of choking and sobbing by Stephanie. Abbie began to feel guilty because she overheard almost all her mother's telephone calls and began to realize that she was hearing herself wishing that each call would end. She was relieved to hear that her aunt had agreed to come round on Saturday to stay in their house to keep her mother company. Her name was Dorothy, and she was a couple of years older than her sister. She was a round ball of a woman with three chins and a critical eye which seldom found any merit in anything she came across. Abbie also felt guilty because of the relief she felt that she would be able to return to work on Monday morning instead of staying home with her mother.

Chapter 23

The international detective sat at his office desk reviewing the information which he possessed in connection with the missing cash from the security firm. He picked up his telephone and dialled the number which the taxi firm had given him for Phil Johnson. As before, the telephone just rang and rang and, in the end, Charlie gave up and replaced the receiver. He made a decision.

He left the building and made his way to his car which was parked nearby. He drove to the local railway station and parked near the taxi rank area where a number of vehicles were parked in a queue waiting for fares who might get off the next train to arrive at the station. A few of the drivers were assembled near their cars sharing a cigarette and chat with each other. Charlie approached them and as cheerfully as he could manage, he engaged them in conversation.

"Hi," he said. "I don't know if any of you know Phil Johnson who drives the black Ford?"

He waited a moment for a response, then with his eyebrows raised he said, "I am an old longstanding customer of his and have always contacted him by telephone but in the last few days he has not answered his phone, so I have become a bit concerned about him. I know you might say, 'why worry, just use another taxi' but it's not like him to never answer his phone. I don't suppose any of you have seen him lately, have you?"

They all looked at each other and all shook their heads. One, who was perhaps the friendliest with Phil said.

"Actually, he's not that fastidious about answering his phone. Sometimes he even drives around without it, he leaves it behind at his home occasionally. If he has answered your calls promptly in the past, I guess you were lucky. He's not very modern and does not use the phone that much. He has a group of regular passengers who he always takes so he does not need to rely on the phone that much. Anyway, he is semi-retired and only works two or three days each week."

"Oh yes, I know that," lied Charlie. "But I can't help worrying about him. I don't suppose you know where he lives. I would like to pop round and knock on his door just to satisfy my concern and make sure he is all right."

The same man said, "He lives in that small cul-de-sac of ex-council houses near the sports ground. Do you know it?"

Charlie said he knew it. "Isn't that what they call poets' corner? All the roads named after a poet?"

"Yes," confirmed the other. "He's in Shelly Road, on the corner next door to the old Methodist Hall."

Charlie gave them all his thanks and said he would call round there just to put his mind at rest. He left them to their conversation and returned to his car. He drove straight round to Shelly Road and parked outside the

Methodist Hall and knocked on the door of the corner property next door. To Charlie it had all the hallmarks of an ex-post-war council property. It was small and made of concrete slabs which had been attached to a wooden frame with slate tiles on the roof. It had a small garden with an equally small garage in it. The whole property looked as though it had received no love and attention for many years. Charlie's knock on the door received no answer. He thought that Phil might be out with a fare and determined that he would return in the late afternoon or early evening when Phil might be more expected to be home. He examined the Methodist Hall which appeared to be locked up as though it had been unoccupied for some time. He went back to his office and gave Des a ring.

"Hi," he said. "Just wondering how your enquiries were going. A bit better than mine I hope for your sake."

"Got some interesting news for you," said Des. "If you are not doing anything else now, I was thinking we could get together in the Jubilee Inn. Is that OK with you?"

"Sure," replied Charlie. "See you there in about fifteen minutes."

He put down his telephone and gave the calendar girl a wink and a nod and then gathered up his coat and briefcase and made his way down the stairs and out of the building and off in the direction of the Jubilee Inn. He arrived, as usual, before Des and was greeted as ever by a rosy faced smiling Reg who reached for a glass and was pouring it before Charlie reached the bar.

"Morning, Charlie," said Reg affably. "Just the one or will Des be joining you today?"

"Yes, he will," replied Charlie, perusing the wall of photographs behind the host. He pointed to one in the top row and pointed to it.

"Who's that, Reg?" he asked squinting his eyes to try to remember someone he felt he should know.

Reg turned to see which photograph Charlie was pointing towards. He smiled knowingly and said to his customer with pride, "That Charlie, is Jeffrey Archer, the famous author, I would have thought that you should have recognised him."

"Oh, yes of course," said Charlie annoyed with himself that he had been forced to ask. "Where did you meet him then?"

"That photo was taken at a book signing occasion in a local bookshop a year or two ago. But I first met him years before. We were at school together."

"Really?" responded Charlie. "What was he like there? Was he obviously a future best-selling author?"

"I don't really know," admitted Reg. "He was in a different class in a different year from me, so I never actually knew him. I can only say that he was there at the same time as me."

Charlie nodded and paid for the two drinks which Reg had poured and took them to his favourite table. He settled down and began to read his Daily Mail. Shortly after he started reading his paper Des arrived and made his way to the bar counter and exchanged greetings with Reg. He perused the lunchtime menu and ordered cottage pie and chips for himself and called out to Charlie who confirmed that he would have the same. Des ordered another drink for his friend as well and paid Reg for everything. He went over to the table where Charlie was seated.

"How's it going then?" he asked. "Any good news?"

"Not really," Charlie told him. "I have had a very unprofitable day trying to track down the taxi driver who took Stephen Pike to the vaccination centre on the day the money disappeared."

He then recalled for Des all the developments in respect of his enquiries, "At least, I have discovered his address," he said. "Although, I have not actually managed to meet up with him yet, and even if I do there is no certainty that the taxi driver will have anything useful to tell us. Still, leave no stone unturned I always say."

"Absolutely," said Des. "That's what I have always liked about you. Well, my enquiries have been a little more successful than yours. I got in touch with a pal of mine who works, or used to work, for the foreign Office security force. He explained to me that there had been some rumours about our friend Jones in Hong Kong when he worked for the security department of the HSBC bank. My concern had always been that since the Chinese takeover of the island, all records of any episodes prior to the take-over date were lost to this side of the universe. However, he assured me that before the take-over all paperwork had been electronically transferred to UK."

"And?" said Charlie. "Or is it a *but*?"

At that moment, their lunches arrived and were served at their table by Reg's wife who had just prepared them in the kitchen. They each chose their condiments from a containerful and were handed their knives and forks each wrapped in a tissue. They each tucked into their cottage pie.

"So," asked Charlie through his mouthful. "Did you manage to find out anything else?"

"And how!" answered Des. "He put me in touch with the head of security in the HSBC bank in this country. He checked all the files they had and told me a few interesting things about Mr Jones. He joined the bank in Hong Kong about ten years ago. Previously, he had worked as a security officer for a large hotel. His duties at the bank required him occasionally to visit the Chinese mainland. That was no problem for him because he spoke the language like a native. His mother was a Chinese lady who married an Englishman who had been in the region with the British forces at the end of the war. The incident that occurred at the bank was the disappearance of a substantial sum of money. It left the bank in the only van that went out of the premises on the day. The CCTV camera at the bank showed the van leaving with two guards in it. One was an older man who had worked at the bank for many years and had family on the island and who after the event had no knowledge or information about the incident.

"The other guard was a much younger man, obviously of Chinese origin who, when they retrospectively checked his prior history before joining the bank, was found to have given false information. After the event he had disappeared and was presumed to have gone to the Chinese mainland. It was concluded that he could not have managed the theft by himself.

"Jones, on the day of itself, was playing a round of golf with the boss of the bank. Detailed enquiries concluded that he was the only member of staff who could have planned or organised the heist, but there was no trace of any solid evidence against him. The money had undoubtedly ended up on the Chinese mainland with the dishonest guard who was clearly a mere assistant. The bank had to accept that there was insufficient evidence to convict Jones and he consistently refused to confess. However, the bank dismissed him with no pension which indicated their judgement of him, whereas his acceptance of the dismissal was as close as they were ever going to get to an admission from him. He returned to the UK, first to take up a job with a security firm in the London area which he left to take up the job which he now holds."

"So," said Charlie. "What we have here is an almost precise copy of what happened in Hong Kong about ten years ago. The only common factor is Jones himself. Clearly, he chose the cleaner as an unwitting accomplice, but he suffered a heart attack and died and so will not be available to point the finger at Jones. The question is, of course, did he have the time and opportunity to hand over the money to Jones?"

"Indeed," conceded Des. "Maybe easier said than done. I will need to go to Stephen Pike's house and have a look round and talk to his sister and get Jones himself to come into the station to be interviewed although I have a funny feeling that he will make no admissions whatsoever."

Charlie agreed with him and said, "And I will have to see If I can track down that taxi driver to see if he can offer any light on things."

They finished their lunch and agreed to continue with their respective tasks and report back to each other as soon as possible.

Chapter 24

Abbie was up first in the morning, even though it had been agreed that she did not need to go into work until Monday at least. She put the kettle on to make a cup of tea for herself and found herself a bowl and then filled it with some cereal. She sat on a stool munching her breakfast without any enthusiasm

Although she was alone, she did not mind. Since the dreadful news of her father's suicide, this was the first moment for her to reflect on the subject without being side-tracked by having to observe and look out for her mother's grief.

She recalled the last time she had seen him the day before and remembered his distant frame of mind and the strange words he had uttered to her when she had asked him what he was thinking about; what was it he had said, "Perhaps the futility of everything."

She recalled at the time that it was an odd choice of words for him to utter but she only realized their relevance now and too late. She cajoled herself for not having appreciated that anything had been worrying him. She also remembered sitting in his shed with him and seeing that single tear rolling down his cheek. Suddenly she felt such sorrow and guilt and sobbed quietly to herself. She kept seeing his face and realized that she should, could, have done more to comfort and assist him. She continued to weep quietly for about ten minutes until she heard approaching steps on the stairs. She dried her eyes as best as she could and pretended to be sorting some cutlery when her mother came into the kitchen.

"Morning, Mum," she said as cheerfully as she could manage. "How are you this morning?"

Stephanie paused for a moment and looked at her and then immediately started crying which prompted Abbie to do the same, indeed she had not really ceased crying from before. They both hugged each other and continued sobbing gently into each other's shoulder. They continued thus for about another five minutes until Dorothy entered the kitchen and started clucking like an old hen. Abbie used her interruption as a prompt to be able to retire to her bedroom, leaving the two sisters to console each other.

For the rest of the morning Stephanie spent most of her time talking on the telephone to anyone whom she had forgotten to speak to the previous day. Abbie remained in her room for most of the morning and would have stayed there all day but for the nagging from her own conscience which forced her to come back downstairs for the odd interval.

In the middle of the afternoon Dorothy managed to get them both together by making a pot of tea and demanding that they both come into the kitchen to drink it. She also found some scones in the fridge which she had spread with butter and insisted that both Abbie and her mother should sit down quietly and put away their mobile telephones for a few minutes. They had each been willing to accede to Dorothy's request and had settled down, each in their own way, content to sit together and converse, when the doorbell rang. Abbie jumped up, feeling perhaps that she should go to answer the door since she had the youngest legs.

She returned to the kitchen a moment later followed closely by the same two police officers who had visited them yesterday. Stephanie introduced them to her sister and invited them to sit down. Dorothy took it upon herself to offer them both a cup of tea which they gratefully accepted.

The male officer, who seemed to be the senior of the two and who certainly did most of the talking, said to Stephanie, "Mrs Wilson, we promised that we would come round to let you know as soon as we had discovered anything which you might wish to know about. As we mentioned yesterday, in circumstances such as yours everything is in the hands of the coroner and it is to him that we will be reporting There can be no action in this matter, which means that no funeral can take place unless and until the coroner knows all the facts and decides. Now, as I told you before we found your husband's telephone which was with him in the car when he was found. Our boffins at the station have been having a look at it and have discovered some disturbing information which will be included in our report to the coroner.

Your husband it would seem had been indulging in some on-line gambling. He used his phone to place bets with one of the on-line betting shops and apparently, he had run up a hefty bill with them. Take a look at this please and tell me if you had any idea that this had been going on."

Here, he held up Percy's phone for Stephanie to see and watched for her reaction. She in turn, looked in horror at the device and the running total bill which was shown on the screen. She put her hands to her face and looked shell-shocked. Abbie looked over her shoulder and was also shocked. She said, not directly to her mother or the policeman, "How can that be possible, when and why would he do this? Did you have any idea about this, Mum?"

"Well, that was going to be my next question Mrs Wilson. Were you aware of any of this? Did your husband gamble often?"

"No, no, no!" said Stephanie emphatically. "Never, as far as I was aware, I have never known him to have any interest in gambling. I am flabbergasted. I don't know what to say. This is even worse than yesterday."

She started to cry again copiously, and Dorothy took her and Abbie in her arms and rocked them as Stephanie wailed. Abbie looked completely shocked and was unable to raise a single tear unlike her mother who it seemed would cry the inevitable ocean.

"Well," said the policeman rising to his feet. "I am so very sorry to bring you this unfortunate news but have to say that the coroner will have to be informed, and will no doubt decide or conclude that your husband's mind was obviously affected by this and judging by the size of the debt, that there was sufficient reason for him to have done what he did. I am sorry."

Both the police officers then took their leave of the ladies and returned to the police station being only too aware of the shock and the misery which they were leaving behind them.

Chapter 25

Phil was up early in the morning and had plenty of time to give his car a spring clean. He gave the inside a vacuum clean and hung a new fresh air device from his rear-view mirror. Then he applied a bucketful of warm water containing washing up liquid enough to produce plenty of suds which he rubbed all over the outside of his vehicle with a large sponge. When that was finished he put away his equipment and got in his car and drove to his first fare.

Beryl was ready for him and as soon his vehicle pulled up outside, she hobbled out to meet him. Phil watched her suffering the pain with every movement. She slumped into his passenger seat and gave a groan. Phil sat down beside her and took a deep breath. He held an envelope in his hands as he said to her, "Well, Beryl, it's Tesco's day today, but before we go there, I want to take you to the office where you pay the money for your operation. I presume it's the private hospital on the hill in Bristol, is it?"

Beryl looked nonplussed and nodded vaguely but looked at Phil with eyes raised.

He passed the envelope to her saying, "In this envelope is sufficient money to pay for your operation and I want you to go there, pay them, and have that operation as soon as possible and change your life around. There is a note included with the cash. It is an anonymous note wishing you well and signed by 'a well-wisher'. You do not need to know where this came from and if anyone asks you any questions you can show them this note and tell them you found it on your doorstep."

Beryl was astounded; she opened the envelope and read the note and glanced at the cash inside. With bewilderment she asked him. "But why are you doing this Phil, where did this money come from?"

"Don't worry about it, Beryl," he said. "I didn't steal it and it couldn't be used for a better purpose. I won't be here much longer to explain any of the questions which people may have. Just remember, you know nothing. Just enjoy it and the rest of your life."

He started the car and drove towards the private clinic in Bristol without giving Beryl any further information. She sat dumb and shell-shocked all the way. When they arrived, Phil parked as close to the entrance door as possible and helped her exit the car and walked her to the doorway but thereafter returned to his car. Whilst he did this he checked carefully to see if there were any CCTV cameras installed at the entrance of the building and noted that there did not appear to be any.

After about thirty minutes Beryl emerged and, again with Phil's help, made her way to the car and settled in the passenger seat. Phil got in beside her and looked at her with raised eyes.

"Well"" he asked. "how did it go?"

Beryl nodded and seemed still dumbstruck. She breathed in deeply and said, "Yeah, it was OK. They accepted the money and I spoke to the surgeon, and it's all arranged for exactly one week from now. I must turn up here with my suitcase and a change of clothes at ten a.m. in the morning and will be staying in the clinic for two or three days and then, if I am recovered well enough, can return home. So, Phil, will you be able to pick me up next week and deliver me here, and then pick me up when it's time for me to go home?"

Phil smiled and nodded. "So, no problem with the cash?"

Beryl shook her head. "No, there did not appear to be any problem. I got the impression that this is not the first time that they have been paid in cash for this sort of operation."

Phil nodded confidently and started the engine of his car.

"Right Beryl, let's get you off to Tesco's for your weekly grocery shop. And after that I have another errand to run, another person to see."

He then drove her to Tesco's and watched as she struggled with her trolly into the store and told himself that this would probably be the last time that he would see her struggling like this. When she returned, he unloaded her shopping trolly and helped her into the car. He drove her home and once he had carried all her shopping from the boot of his car into her kitchen but today, because he had somewhere else to go, he had to forego his usual cup of coffee with Beryl.

"Well," he said. "I have to be off now but I will arrive here in seven days' time at nine a.m. which will give us sufficient time to get to the clinic in time for your appointment. So, make sure you are ready with your suitcase packed, OK?"

Beryl confirmed that she would be ready and waiting and once again thanked him profusely for providing the cash which would make so much difference to her life. Phil then drove off and made his way to Oswald's place. He parked outside the front steps just by Oswald's basement and went down the steps and knocked on his door.

Oswald opened the door and asked Phil to come in and wait while he changed his clothes before they went on their journey. He sat down in a chair waiting for Ossie and produced from his pocket an envelope like the one he had given to Beryl. When Oswald re-appeared, he presented him with the envelope and an identical note signed by a well-wisher. He explained to him, in the same way that he had explained to Beryl, that he (Oswald) would tell anyone who asked that the envelope had been dropped on his mat and that he had seen nobody, and he also knew nothing.

Like Beryl before him, Oswald was totally amazed by Phil's announcement but was not quite as diffident as Beryl had been. True, the cost of a laser operation on his cataracts was not nearly as expensive as the hip operation for Beryl, but Oswald was not nearly so squeamish about receiving such help and was very optimistic about the outcome and expressed many thanks to Phil for his generous offer and appeared to feel no guilt about accepting his offer. As if to explain his position he said, "Thanks a million, Phil. If our roles were reversed, I would do the same for you."

Phil told him that he believed him, and they both moved outside and got into Phil's car and began their journey. They went through the same procedure as Phil had carried out with Beryl and similarly Oswald got an early appointment for his laser operation. When their journeys were complete, and Phil brought him back home he re-iterated what he had told Oswald about the secrecy or lack of knowledge as to where the money for the operation had come from.

"Don't worry," he told Oswald. "I did not steal the money, although it was never mine, but if someone ever traces the cash back to you, as long as you show them my note and maintain your story you will be safe."

Oswald repeated his thanks and Phil drove back to his home.

Chapter 26

Des sat in his office and reflected on what he had discovered about Mr Jones. He telephoned through to the general office and asked for his sergeant to join him. Seconds later the sergeant appeared and sat down. Des showed him the folder he had on his desk and asked him what knowledge he had of the security company.

"Nothing really," he said. "They have been in existence for ten or fifteen years and never come to our attention at all. We went down there when the disappearance of the money was reported. We looked at their CTTV camera which showed their cleaner leaving the place shortly after the delivery van. The cleaner, as you know, ended up at the vaccination centre where he got taken ill and was rushed to the hospital in an ambulance but later died. The hospital said he had had a heart attack and I guess they are the experts; they should know. When he died no money was found either at the hospital or at the vaccination centre. Uniform branch has done a search of both areas but found not a trace of that backpack he was carrying when he was filmed leaving the security firm premises. It is presumed that the cash was inside it, although we do not know that for certain. Neither do we know where the backpack is whether empty or full of cash."

Des brought him up to date on the enquiries he had made into Mr Jones and asked him if he had ever met the man or knew anything about him.

"No," replied the sergeant. "Never heard of him except I know he was the man who first advised us about the loss of the money."

"That's right," said Des. "I've seen the interview between himself, and a young lady called Abbigail at the solicitors, Featherstones, whom the firm has instructed to act for them in the search for the money. She seems to me to be a discerning young lady and she said she thought he looked slimy and suspicious and having watched the video I am inclined to agree with her."

"But why?" asked the sergeant. "Did they decide to employ a firm of solicitors to look into this matter?

"Good question," said Des. "I asked the same question and the answer seems to be; (a), they don't fully trust us, and (b), they feel they need to be legally represented if and when the money is found."

"Hmm," said the sergeant unconvinced, with a look of disbelief on his face. "Sounds slightly fishy to me."

"I know," replied Des. "I feel the same. I think it is time we had a little chat with Mr Jones. In view of the information contained in here (he waved the folder he had previously referred to), this robbery is a carbon copy of the one that took place at the HSBC bank about ten years ago. There is no doubt in my mind that he was responsible for the whole operation. Our only problem will be joining up the dots."

"Yeah, I agree," said the sergeant. "It really is too similar to be a mere coincidence, and the decision to appoint a firm of solicitors to help with the search just seems snide and superfluous."

"Yes," agreed Des. "You are right, but what he does not know is that the solicitors, in order to discover everything, they could, decided to employ a private detective to help them. Guess who they instructed?"

The sergeant squinted with concentration, then smiled knowingly and pointed his finger at Des with a triumphant gesture, "Charlie Chivers?"

Des smiled back at him with equal elation.

"The very same," he said. "Right, let's you and I go and have a little chat with our Mr Jones."

They both drove out to the security firm premises and parked in the 'visitor's' car parking space. Before entering the building, they viewed the garage area on the end. It was a large area about the size of a triple garage and had a steel shuttering in place that rolled up and down powered by an electric motor. The closed shuttered doorway was the one that had been shown on the CCTV camera view from the inside of the premises and had shown the cleaner Stephen Pike leaving the property with a backpack on. When they had finished looking at the garage, they entered the building and announced themselves at the reception desk and requested an interview with Mr Jones.

After a few minutes the man himself came down the staircase from the first floor and walked over to them. They were seated on the visitors' chairs leafing through some fashion magazines that were scattered on a circular table. As they watched him approach from the foot of the stairway Des thought how suave and stylish, he appeared to be. It was like watching Fred Astaire gliding across a dance floor to take the hand of Ginger Rogers. He wore a quality suit of a pale pastel blue colour and although he was at least fifty years of age he still looked trim and fit.

"Good morning, gentlemen," he said. "What can I do to help you?"

Des showed him his warrant card and introduced himself and his sergeant as they both got to their feet.

"Good day to you, Mr Jones. We were hoping to have a word with you about the matter of the missing money. I hope it's not an inconvenient time."

"Not at all," he said with a charming smile, and after a brief pause said. "But perhaps a phone call warning of your arrival would have been polite and helpful. I am a very busy man and am often elsewhere meeting with people."

"Well, point taken," said Des cheerfully. "But it is our experience that if we announce our visits to people, when we arrive, most of them are not there."

He gave a chuckle as if to imply that this was not really a serious conversation, "But anyway, we are here now so perhaps we could have a word or two?"

Mr Jones led them up the stairway to his office on the first floor. He indicated the chairs for them to sit down upon and took up his place behind his desk. Behind him was a bookcase containing three shelves full of a variety of books and on the top were a number of photographs, two or three of which appeared to be taken abroad somewhere. One of the photographs was a Chinese lady stood on a harbour in front of some impressive looking boats. Des presumed the photograph was probably taken in Hon Kong.

"So, Mr Jones," he began. "Can you please tell us exactly what happened on the day the money went missing."

"Well," he responded. "I don't think there is anything I have to say that I haven't already told your officers the other day."

"Of course," said Des. "But if you would kindly indulge us, it would be helpful if you could go through it again today."

Mr Jones breathed in deeply and struggled not to roll his eyes. Des thought he had the look about him of a David Niven character in a film he had seen. A stylish colonial with a pencil moustache and a confident air.

"Well, as I said before, the money was stored in a secure room, and it was not known when exactly it was removed. A subsequent enquiry by use of our CCTV system showed our cleaner leaving the premises via the garage area carrying a backpack in which presumably the money was stored."

"And what did you do then?" asked Des.

"Well, phoned you, naturally," he replied. "You must have a record of when that was done surely?"

"Yes, of course," said Des. "But we have to go over every point just to be sure we understand what exactly happened. Was it you who phoned the police?"

"Yes, it was," he replied.

"I see," said Des, who already knew that having checked the point before leaving the station. "And are you in charge of this establishment?"

"No," was the response. "I am the deputy manager. The manager is Mr Wilkinson but he has been away at our head office in Swindon for the last two weeks."

"And how long have you been at this establishment, Mr Jones?"

"Oh, about ten years," was the reply

"And where did you work before you came here?" asked the sergeant.

"I was in Hong Kong for a number of years, I worked for a large hotel and later for a bank."

"So, what made you decide to return to this country?" asked Des.

"Aah well," he replied, stroking his moustache with an index finger. "The political climate dictated that it was time for me to come home. I love the far East but was not prepared to live under the regime of the present Chinese government. The place is no longer independent, and no longer suitable for me to live in. I have many friends and acquaintances who either chose to stay there or had no choice, and I feel so sorry for them. Life, I'm afraid, will never be the same again for those in Hong Kong."

"And so," said the sergeant artfully. "If it had not been for the Chinese takeover of the island, you would still be out there now?"

"Oh absolutely," he replied. "I would never have otherwise left the island. It was always like paradise for me."

Des looked across to the bookcase, and the photograph of a Chinese lady sitting in a silver frame.

"And is that photograph taken in Hong Kong?" he asked

"Yes," he replied. "That is my mother, she is Chinese herself. My father served in the forces in that region, and they met there and married."

"And did she, I wonder, come back with you to UK?"

"No regrettably, she has too large a family to leave. We are still in touch of course, but things will never be the same again."

"But surely," said the sergeant. "You must have aspirations to return there at some time, is your father still alive?"

"No, he died a few years ago," he said, wiping at one eye with a finger although Des noticed that there was not a trace of a tear in that eye.

"And what can you tell us about the cleaner eh, Mr Pike?" Des asked.

"Well, not an awful lot I'm afraid. He was, I believe, a single man who kept very much to himself, I never really got to know him. I certainly did not ever appreciate that he was cunning and dishonest."

"What can you tell us about that?" asked Des with interest.

"Oh, several incidents of items going missing from my office," he replied. "Some small amounts of cash in my desk drawer and a watch which I had bought in Hong Kong, a flashy looking fake Rolex which was not very expensive, but it looked as if it was. Nothing I could ever prove but I was pretty sure that it was him. Being the cleaner he had access to all rooms and could never be challenged."

"Well, anyway," said Des rising to his feet. "Perhaps you would be good enough to show us around the premises and the garage area while we are here."

Mr Jones gave them a guided tour of the whole building and garage and when they had finished Des told him that they had seen enough for now, "I know you told us that you were not planning to return to Hong Kong, but in any event (here he chuckled wryly), please don't leave the country until we have finished our investigations."

Chapter 27

Abbie was awake early on Monday morning and had already, before rising, had decided to go to work. She sat in the kitchen munching some muesli and milk with a cup of green tea. Her mother entered the kitchen wearing a dressing gown and looking frankly dreadful.

Her husband's suicide had been such an enormous shock for her. It not only gave her a sense of loss, but a feeling that she had, perhaps, never fully known or understood him. More particularly she became aware that he had undoubtedly been harbouring concerns or worries which she had never discerned and for this she felt great guilt. She was still struggling to come to terms with the events which she feared or knew would always be a presence in her life.

Abbie was also struggling badly with their mutual loss but still felt that she was incapable of reconciling both her own and her mother's problems at the same time. She watched her mother slopping around the kitchen in her pyjamas and slippers and knew that she was relieved to be leaving the house shortly to go to work. She gave her mother a silent embrace and then washed up her cereal bowl and reached for her coat and gave her mother a farewell kiss.

"You'll be all right with Dorothy, won't you?" she asked as she made her way to the front door.

"Hmm," mumbled her mother as she closed the door behind her.

When she arrived at work everyone was very sympathetic and understanding. Mr Morris was especially solicitous about her presence in the office and assured her that if she had any worries or concerns then she only had to tell him, and he would be pleased to allow her time off work. She reminded him that she had a class at the college later in the morning so she would only be in the office for an hour or so. He assured her that that would be all right and he hoped the class would be a distraction for her. After an hour and a bit of reviewing her files and dictating a few letters and checking a few items in the modest office library, she gathered up her briefcase with class notes, her handbag and raincoat, she left the building and made her way to her car which was parked nearby and drove to the college. She was relieved to see Maisie was there and sat beside her and resolved to have lunch with her later. The morning lecture was on the subject of Torts which was something that had always interested her. In her bedroom the night before, she had been browsing through the subject in her book and had read with interest all about the famous case of Rylands v Fletcher and it's equally famous judgement which commenced with the words, "We think that the law is that if anyone collects or brings onto his land anything that is likely to do harm…" Abbie could not remember the name of the judge.

When lunchtime arrived, much to Abbie's relief, Mavis agreed to go for lunch with her to a nearby coffee house. As they settled down to eat and drink Mavis, in her usual chirpy way, asked Abbie if she was all right. Abbey looked blankly ahead for a few moments and then suddenly all the tears began to roll down her cheeks and she finally muttered, "My dad committed suicide last Thursday."

Mavis was horrified and paused for a second then put down her fork and spoon, and moved over to the bench Abbie was occupying and sat beside her and took her in her arms and said, "Oh my god Abbie, how awful. Please tell me about it if you can."

They both sat together arm in arm while Abbie sobbed out her story and Maisie also began to cry, "Oh Abbie, I can't tell you how sorry I am. But what are you doing here, surely you should be home with your mother shouldn't you?"

Abbie explained that her aunt Dorothy was there with her mother and there was nothing extra that she (Abbie), could add to the situation.

"To be honest," she said. "I feel riddled with guilt because I can't give my mum the solace she needs and deserves, but also," she sobbed again. "I realized too late a couple of warning signs which my dad gave me, and I never noticed them for what they were." Again, she burst into another fit of sobbing as she stammered out, "I was not there for him when he needed someone. I was so busy thinking of myself that I never even noticed the signs which to me are now obvious."

"There, there," said Maisie smoothing her head gently. "You must not blame yourself for what happened. It was not your fault Abbie, your dad was not well and there was nothing you could have done to avoid what happened. Sometimes in such circumstances people are unable to speak out or reach out for help and no matter how close one is, it is not possible to see the bigger picture. Do not blame yourself, you have done nothing wrong."

They both stayed in each other's arms for about five minutes and finally Abbie's tears ceased to fall and she admitted to Maisie, "This is the first time I have really cried."

Mavis patted her shoulder and said, "It's good for you to cry and it's nothing to feel ashamed of. We cannot go back to class like this. Let's stay here and talk more about this and you can tell me more about how you are feeling."

And that is what they did. They ordered more coffee and some cream cakes and Abbie told her all about the tell-tale signs that she had retrospectively spotted in her dad and also the on-line gambling which the police had detected on his telephone. Maisie was astonished by the whole outpouring and assured her that if it had been her instead of Abbie, she would have made the same mistakes.

Eventually, they both decided that it was time to go home, and Maisie insisted that they both exchange telephone numbers and that Abbie should phone her, any time, day or night, if she was feeling down. Abbie promised that she would and thanked her for being so sympathetic.

Chapter 28

Charlie sat in his office reviewing the information which he and Des had unearthed but had to admit to himself that they had got no further forward. He was going over in his mind the interview that had occurred between them and Mr Jones. He concluded that the original assessment of the man by Abbie had been spot on. To him the fellow came across as duplicitous and self-serving.

He knew, from what Des had told him, that Jones had been dismissed by the HSBC bank in Hong Kong before returning to the UK. During the interview he had led them to believe that his only reason for leaving the island had been the imminence of the Chinese take-over Whilst he had to admit that no one would readily reveal that he had been sacked from a job, the co-incidental nature of the event in Hong Kong and the similar occurrence at the security firm premises, made Jones' failure to mention it much more than a mere oversight. He felt that Jones would have reasoned that due to the Chinese take-over of the island all previous records would have been lost for ever and therefore he could hide any of the true facts about his past. He had no doubt that Jones would never voluntarily offer the true details of his previous employment.

He was also interested in the gratuitous way in which he had described the cleaner's alleged theft(s) from his office. He figured that once the cleaner's death had been announced Jones felt confident to invent any story which might lend suspicion to the deceased as to his involvement in the theft of the money.

Charlie reminded himself that he ought to return to the property of Stephen Pike to make some further enquiries of his sister. He felt that the information he had acquired from his sister had painted a very different character from the person Mr Jones had sought to portray. He knew that he needed to gather some more information but first he felt that he needed a pint of his favourite ale. He picked up his phone and dialled the number of the police station where Des was stationed.

"Hi, it's me," he said. "Are you up for a drink and a chat?"

"Sure am," replied Des. "I was just about to phone you. See you there in about fifteen minutes."

Charlie loaded up his aged brief case with his notes, his pens and the Daily Mail and then picked his coat up from the spare chair where he had earlier deposited it, and, with a silent farewell bid to the calendar girl, made his way downstairs. As he reached the bottom of the stairs, he encountered Mavis coming out of the offices of Huw Roberts & Co. They greeted each other and strolled together to the pavement outside and spoke briefly to each other.

"How's it going, Charlie? Are you busy today, how are the enquiries coming along with that security firm case?"

"Oh, coming on," he replied. "But not complete yet, but my money is on that slippery so and so, Jones."

"Ah," she said, with some satisfaction. "Why am I not surprised?"

She then briefly told him the dire news about Abbie's father. Charlie was very sorry to hear that and said that if she saw Abbie again soon, to pass on his good wishes.

"I'm just off to meet Des in the Jubilee Inn," he told her. "I'm hoping he may have some information for me."

"Oh really," she said. "Good luck with that, keep me updated."

She walked off one way and Charlie went the other towards the Jubilee Inn. He entered the bar room and found Reg, the landlord behind the bar as usual drying some glasses with a dish cloth.

"Morning, Charlie," he said cheerfully reaching for a pint glass and beginning to draw down the ale. "Will it be just a pint for you today, or will you be taking lunch today? My good lady has made a cottage pie today. Interested?"

"Absolutely," he responded. "How could I resist one of your wife's delicious cottage pies? I will definitely have one thank you and you had better make it two please because Des will be here in a minute. I know he will want one as well. Make it two pints as well please, Reg."

The landlord poured both glasses and Charlie paid and sat down at his usual table. He rummaged into his briefcase and extracted the Daily Mail and began reading while he sipped his beer. In less than five minutes Des arrived and was greeted at the bar by Reg who was pleased to announce to him that both drinks and two cottage pies with chips had already been ordered, and paid for, by Charlie.

"That's what I love to hear Reg, I'd better go and join him." He moved across the room to the table where Charlie was seated.

"Morning Charlie, how are you today?"

"Very well thanks," he replied. "I just bumped into Mavis as I was leaving the office and she was telling me that the father of the young lady, Abbigail, who instructed me on this security firm robbery case, had committed suicide the other day. How sad is that?"

"Oh God," said Des. "That is so unfortunate, how did he choose to do it?"

"Well," he said. "Apparently, he drove out to the waste land up on the hill near the woods and attached a hose pipe to his car exhaust. He was found by a dog walker and the uniform branch at your station were summoned."

"Wow," reflected Des. "How does any family get over that? It would be bad enough to be told your husband or father had been run over but that is a whole different level. That poor girl."

"Yes," agreed Charlie. "So, have you got any news for me?"

"Well, as a matter of fact I have, but it will have to wait a few minutes while I concentrate on my cottage pie which is just arriving."

Charlie looked over his shoulder to see Reg's wife approaching with a tray full of cottage pies and cutlery and condiments. They both gave a sigh of satisfaction as their plates were placed before them.

"Hmm, that looks really appetising," said Des, enthusiastically. "Thank you so much."

"Yes," echoed Charlie. "Thank you very much."

"You are both welcome," said Reg's wife and left them to it. They both tucked in and finished off the food by gulping down their beers. Des got to his feet saying, "Same again?"

Charlie nodded and watched as Des moved to the bar and ordered two more beers and chatted with Reg. Soon he returned to the table and set down a beer for Charlie and sat down saying, "One of those bank notes turned up you know."

"Really?" said Charlie raising his eyebrows. "Where from?"

"That lock and key, ironmongery shop off the town square. Do you know it?"

Charlie nodded and asked, "Have you spoken to the shopkeeper yet?"

Des nodded. "Yeah, but no result I'm afraid. In the first place the shopkeeper can't definitely remember, but if it was the guy he thinks it might have been, he cannot give an accurate description. The person he thinks might have passed the note had been wearing a Covid mask and sunglasses."

"Hmm," said Charlie. "More than likely a local then otherwise why would he disguise himself like that unless he thought he might be recognised."

"Yeah, probably," agreed Des. "But whatever his motives with such disguise, we would be hard pressed to take any suspect to court without a full admission. If we did so, then a defence barrister would drive a coach and horses between any prosecution which we brought."

"But what did the suspect buy with the single bank note?" wondered Charlie.

"Well, I understand he bought a locking device for a large up and over garage door."

"Really make any sense, does it."

Des agreed, "Yes, you are right. But of course, he may not yet have spent the rest of the money. We will have to wait and see if any of the other bank notes are passed and if so where that leads us."

Chapter 29

Stephanie had received another visit from the police who were keen to keep her fully in the picture with regard to all their enquiries. The same two officers who she had seen before, came back to see her and explain to her that all their investigations had been concluded and that their report had been made to the coroner. They read to her in detail the whole of their report and advised her of a date of the coroner's hearing which would be taking place in a just under a month's time.

Part of the detail of the report, which upset Stephanie the most, was the information as to the quantity of the debt which her husband had left to the gaming company with whom he had been gambling on the telephone. The total debt was just over £80,000.00. This information was, for Stephanie, staggering. She was shocked and astounded to hear the size of his debt and only then appreciated the size of the problem which her husband had been suffering with.

She broke down in tears, and the police officers were relieved that her sister Dorothy was staying at the house at this time and was available to console her. As delicately as possible they took their leave and assured her that they would be present and able to speak to her further at the coroner's coming hearing. They diplomatically suggested to her that if she had a family solicitor, she might wish to instruct him or her to be present with her at the coroner's hearing.

Stephanie told them tearfully that the last time her husband and she had used a solicitor was about twenty years ago when they had purchased the house, she now lived in. She did however advise them that her daughter worked in the office of a firm of solicitors and that she was at work this day. She told them that she would discuss the matter with her daughter when she returned home.

Later the same day when Abbie came home from work, she sat down with her mother to listen to everything which the police had told her. Like her mother she too was shocked at the amount of the debt which her father had run up with the gaming company. She was also overcome with sorrowful feelings and could not restrain herself from copious sobbing and tears. She asked her mother if she had any previous knowledge of her father's interest in gambling. Stephanie replied that she never had any such knowledge but that, to her knowledge, it must have been a recently acquired interest since she had never discerned such a hobby or interest on her father's behalf.

"So, he was never a habitual gambler throughout his lifetime?" suggested Abbie. "And therefore it must be assumed that it was only recently that he began gambling. How long ago did he acquire his telephone?"

"About five or six years ago," Stephanie replied. "He did not get it until he retired."

"Hmm," muttered Abbie. "So he must have been suffering from some kind of illness for a year or two which made it possible for him to indulge in the hobby or sickness of gambling. Did you ever discern any symptoms of his illness?"

"No," she answered. "None whatsoever, never."

Abbie was not really surprised to hear this. She knew her mother's character well, and appreciated that, as long as she was happy and content, she would never have felt over-solicitous about her husband's welfare as long as he did not show any obvious signs of mental distress. She recalled again her own recent points of concern about her father's mental state which she genuinely believed that her mother would not have noticed.

Later when she was on her own in her bedroom, she determined that she needed to discuss things with someone else other than her mother. She dialled the number which Mavis had kindly entered into her mobile telephone.

"Hello," said Mavis' voice. "How can I help you, Abbie?"

Initially there was no voice at the other end of the telephone, although Mavis knew it was Abbie's number because the entry on her screen told her. Slowly and gradually, Abbie's sobs could be heard down the line and Mavis allowed her two or three minutes of quiet sobbing before saying as gently as she could.

"Would you like to meet up and have a chat, my love? We are not far apart, can I come to you, or would you like to come here?"

Abbie paused for a breath and said, "I am not sure what I want, I just don't know what to do or think. When I dialled your number, I was not intending to impose on you, I just needed to speak to someone. I can't talk to mum about it."

"Quite understandable, Abbie. You must come round here and talk as long as you like."

She gave Abbie her address and post code and general directions and said she would see her in about twenty minutes. Abbie said OK and immediately felt a surge of relief to know that she would be able to share her troubles or concerns with someone else. She dried her eyes and checked herself in the mirror, combed her hair quickly and made her way downstairs and told her mother and Dorothy that she was going out for a while to visit a friend.

In about half an hour she drove up the driveway of Maisie and George's house and parked next to a delightful looking Victorian conservatory. She rang the doorbell which was answered by a pleasant looking young man who smiled discerningly.

"You must be Abbie," he said with some sympathy. "I'm George, Mavis is expecting you, please follow me."

He led Abbie into the house and through the lounge in which there was a TV set on which a football match was being shown. He led her on through into the conservatory in which Mavis was seated upon a cane chair.

Mavis rose and hugged and kissed her and said, "Please have a seat." Indicating a matching cane sofa with cushions on it. "Would you like something to drink?"

Abbie stared in wonder at the conservatory in which she was standing She shrugged off her coat and sat down on the sofa and said, "What a beautiful room this is and what a lovely house you have. I'm driving, so any non-alcoholic drink would be nice thank you."

Mavis disappeared into the kitchen and prepared two lemonades with lime and ice cubes and returned and gave one to Abbie who said again, "This conservatory really is so beautiful. It turns your wonderful house into a palace."

"Thank you," said Mavis. "It is recently built, we got married in here and at the same time two other couples were also married at the same time. It was the most magical day of my life. George has gone back into the lounge to watch a football match, so we have all evening to chat as long as you wish."

She then listened for about half an hour while Abbie told her all about her father's death and his gambling problem which neither she nor her mother knew anything about. She found it a very distressing tale to listen to. By merely re-telling her story Abbie caused herself to start crying again and even Mavis who was used to hearing tales of woe found that she had a lump in her throat and a tear in her eye.

"I am so sorry to come here and to start crying again," said Abbie. "It's just that I don't know what to do or who to talk to."

"Well," said Mavis with great surety. "You may not know who to talk to, but I certainly do."

She got her notebook and made a few notes therein and then said, I know the most wonderful barrister in the country who has been a good friend to me during my articles period. In fact, without a generous reference from her I would never have got a chance to be working my articles. She is an absolutely brilliant barrister and I know she will be able to give us some good advice. Are you up for it?"

Abbie said she supposed she was, and Mavis' face lit up.

"I promise that you won't be sorry," she said. "I will talk to Phillipa Fry (that's her name), and then I'll be in touch with you."

Chapter 30

Phil woke late and remembered that he did not have any fares today that were booked in. He also recalled that both Beryl and Oswald would probably still be recovering from their operations. Phil was quite relieved that he had no work today because he found, when he woke up, that he did not feel very well today. He had a sore throat which would not go away, and his back ached as well as almost all the muscles in his body. As he walked around his house, he felt pains in many parts of his body.

He went into his bathroom and examined himself in the mirror and was amazed at how much weight he had lost in recent weeks. He also noticed, as he gazed into the mirror, that his own complexion had turned from his usual tint into a dismal grey colour. He wondered when this change had taken place and why he had not previously seen it coming. As he moved around, he felt the pain again in his back. He wondered what organ was in that region. He guessed perhaps it was the kidneys and had to hold his position to stem the pain.

He felt a cough coming on and could not help himself. He coughed strongly and felt the soreness in his throat and the pain in almost every part of his body. He tried hard not to cough at all but could not stop the urge and felt the pain wracking his whole body.

He recalled when the surgeon Mr Khan had given him his verdict on his illness. When he diagnosed the prostate cancer and told Phil, he was very kind and gentle about the way in which he carefully told him about the likely symptoms and the time they would take to take over his body. That was about eighteen months ago. The surgeon told him that there was nothing certain about anything, but he gently advised him that he could expect not much more than a year of reasonable health before the symptoms became clear and obvious. He had told Phil to return and see him if and when he began to suffer from the symptoms, he had described so that he could check him out and give him any treatment which was appropriate.

Phil thought about it and knew in his soul that the time had come. He telephoned the number of Mr Khan's office and spoke to a nice lady who said she would speak to Mr Khan and come back to him as soon as possible. He wondered what to do with himself today and decided that the answer was, nothing. He felt so weak and under par that he could not face doing any work at all. He was just considering going back to bed for a lie down and perhaps a further doze, when his phone rang. He answered the call and found that it was Mr Khan's secretary who told him, "I spoke to Mr Khan, who said that a vacancy had arisen in his diary and so he would be pleased to see you hear tomorrow if you could get here. He did say that he thought it was important that you should come and see him as soon as possible. Could you manage that? Say about nine-thirty a.m.?"

Phil confirmed that he would be there the following day.

Sure enough, the next morning Phil was there on time and was greeted by an assistant surgeon or nurse who told him they would like to do one or two tests before Mr Khan would see him. They took some tests including blood and breathing and temperature and rounded it all off with a complete body scan. Thereafter he was shown into a waiting room where he was given a cup of tea and a biscuit.

After about ten minutes Mr Khan arrived and sat with him and spoke to him gently and sympathetically, "Good morning, Mr Johnson. It is good to see you again. The tests we have just carried out have shown that the prediction which I made when I last saw you has come true. I can tell just from your appearance that your health has regressed but the tests have proved beyond doubt that the cancer has spread throughout your body and unfortunately has gone into your bones. I think the time has come for you to go into our 'end of life' centre where you will be made as comfortable as possible."

Phil nodded silently and then thought for a moment before saying, "Yeah, I expected that you would say that. I have not been feeling too great lately."

"Well," he said in as kindly a way as he could manage. "These hard times that we are all living in are not kind to us. One of the tests we carried out has shown that you have contracted Covid. It was not surprising to hear, since the nature of this latest disease is that it homes in upon anyone who is weakened in any way with another complaint. I am so sorry to give you this extra bad news but can assure you that our clinic will make your final weeks as comfortable as possible."

Phil did not know what to say in response.

"I will leave you in the hands of my nurses who will make the arrangements for your entry to the clinic," said Mr Khan who got to his feet and shook his hand and then left him. One of the nurses then took him into an office to arrange for his entry in a couple of weeks or so. She wrote the time and date on a card and gave it to him and reminded him to advise any close relatives of the address.

"Do you have a wife or partner, Mr Johnson?"

"No," he said. "She died about twenty years ago. I have a son and a daughter who live locally."

"Aah, yes," she said. "Well, they may have as much access to you whilst you are in the clinic."

Chapter 31

The international detective woke up with a positive frame of mind. It was a weekend so he figured that the sister of Stephen Pike the cleaner at the security firm, would probably not be at work today. Charlie guessed that she might be at her brother's house and, if so, it might be worth his while to call round and see her again.

He drove to the house and sure enough when he rang the doorbell she answered it.

"Oh," she said with surprise. "I was not expecting a visit from anyone today."

"I know," said Charlie apologetically. "I thought as it was the weekend and you would not be at work, that it might be a good time to call round and catch you."

She invited him in, and they sat down in the lounge which she was in the middle of cleaning.

"I just wanted to get a second look at your brother's character, and which might assist us in our investigations. I have still not managed to locate the taxi driver who took your brother to the vaccination centre. I don't suppose you have any idea about that chap, do you?"

The sister shook her head and had a think.

"Not really," she said. "He usually walked or biked to work, I was never aware that he knew any taxi drivers. As far as I know, the only acquaintances he had were those he met when he went fishing. There is a photograph of him with one man while fishing, I don't suppose that would be of any interest to you?"

Charlie nodded so she hurried into the bedroom and came back with a photograph which she showed to him. The photograph showed two men standing by a riverbank together and smiling into the camera. The younger man at the front was proudly holding a large fish which had obviously just been caught. That man was the cleaner Stephen Pike. The man behind him, also smiling, and with an arm affectionately around the shoulder of his companion was none other than Mr Jones the deputy manager of the security firm.

Charlie looked at the photograph carefully and said to the man's sister, "No, that is no taxi driver, that is Mr Jones the deputy manager of the firm where your brother used to work. I would be very grateful if I could borrow this photograph. I know that my colleague the DCI at the local police station will be very interested to see this. I will make sure this is returned to you when all the investigations are completed."

The sister said he could keep the photograph because she had plenty of other pictures she would prefer to retain. Charlie thanked her for the photograph and her time and then left her and went back to his office to consider matters further. When he was seated at his desk, he reviewed what he had already discovered. "What else is there for me to do?" he wondered and then realized that there was something he had left undone.

"Of course," he said to himself. "It's time for me to visit Mr Phil Johnson."

His previous experience of telephoning Phil had proved so unsuccessful that he decided to try a personal visit again. He got to his car and breathed a sigh of relief when it started straight away. He drove to the house of Phil Johnson and parked outside of the Methodist Hall and stepped out of the car to see a black Ford parked on the forecourt of Phil's house. He walked up to the front door and rang the bell. After what seemed like an eternity the door was opened by a bleary-eyed Phil who looked as though he had been awoken in the middle of the night.

"Phil Johnson?" said Charlie expectantly. Phil did not answer, he just stared at Charlie as if he were still slumbering.

"Charlie Chivers," said Charlie, fishing out a card which he handed to Phil. "I'm helping the police with a few enquiries they are making about the death of an unfortunate man who worked at the security firm down on the industrial estate. Mind if I come in for a few minutes?"

Phil stood back to admit the detective and then preceded him into the kitchen. A perfunctory glance around him was enough to tell Charlie that the whole place needed a bit of spit and polish.

"I was wondering if you remember taking a guy named Stephen Pike to the vaccination centre. I don't know if you know, but he had a heart attack there and was taken to the hospital where he died?"

"Yeah, I heard that," he said. "But I didn't really know him, I just took him to the centre and when he didn't come out and I asked one of the helpers, I was told he had been taken to the hospital by ambulance."

"So, he wasn't one of your regular fares?"

"No, I just picked him up in the town square by accident almost and just took him there and then never saw him again. I didn't know him."

"Do you remember if he had a backpack or the like when he got into your taxi?" asked Charlie.

Phil shook his head. "I don't remember," he said.

Charlie nodded and glanced around the kitchen as he asked, "Have you no fares today, are you not busy?"

"No," he said stroking his own tired face. "I have not been too well lately, so am taking a day off for a bit of a rest."

"OK," said Charlie getting to his feet as if to leave, he paused to read a label on a box on the work top. "Hmm," he said slowly reading the label. "Garage door locking device eh, Going to be doing some DIY jobs today, eh?"

Phil looked grey and tired and admitted, "Nah, I think I may go back to bed."

"Yeah well," said Charlie making his way out into the hall and letting himself out of the front door. Turning round he said to Phil, "Sorry to have interrupted your nap, hope you feel better soon."

Phil gave a wry smile and closed the door.

Chapter 32

The coroner's court was on the outside of town; it was once a small hospital which had been transformed into its present state. There did not appear to be too many people in attendance. There were the two police officers who had called at Stephanie's house. Stephanie had instructed her solicitor to attend on her behalf, although she did not really feel that he was her personal solicitor because she did not even know or recognise him. She merely instructed the firm who had last represented herself and Percy when they purchased their house. She instructed the firm over the telephone and the first time she met him was on the morning of the hearing in the courtyard outside. He looked about twenty-three years old and admitted when they met, that he had never been to this court before. Stephanie thought he looked like a schoolboy.

When the hearing commenced the coroner entered the courtroom and the hearing was in session. She was a middle-aged lady who glanced at her notes, and the people in the courtroom over the top of a pair of fancy looking purple-shaded glasses which reminded Abbie of Dame Edna Everidge, the character played by the Australian comedian Barry Humphries.

Unlike Dame Edna, the coroner never said anything amusing or ironic. She seemed to be content to listen attentively to everything that was said by each witness and to make constant notes. At the end of each witness' evidence she did at least have the courtesy to ask Stephanie's solicitor if he had any questions, but it seemed that usually he could not think of any questions to ask except when the doctor who had been summoned by the police to examine Percy's body when it was discovered in his car, he did ask him how long he estimated that it would have taken him to die. Presumably he was hoping to achieve with this question a reply that death would have been quite quick, and therefore be of some comfort for his client Stephanie, but in fact the doctor winced and stated that it was very difficult to be precise on that point but guessed that he had probably lingered in the car for anything up to several hours, which was neither exact nor of any comfort to Stephanie.

When all the witnesses had been heard the coroner took a ten-minute break while everyone sat around in the courtroom waiting and Stephanie sobbed bitterly.

Then the coroner came back into the court room and delivered her judgement. She spoke for about twenty minutes or so. During the first half of her speech, she seemed to utter a precis of each piece of evidence which had just been delivered by the witnesses themselves. In the second half of her judgement, she confined herself to delivering a heartrending description of the effect that the manner of Percy's death would no doubt have had upon anyone involved in the whole sorry procedure. As if to emphasize her words Stephanie sobbed quietly throughout the whole of her judgement which she concluded by saying that Percy's death occurred during a period in which his mind was deranged and that was probably due to the fact that he had run up gambling debts on his telephone, but no doubt could have been due to other personal problems with which he had been dealing personally but had decided not to discuss with anyone. She wished the family of the deceased good fortune at an understandably tragic time.

The hearing was over, and everyone trooped out of the courtroom and almost everybody else who had been in the courtroom all shuffled past Stephanie to offer their sympathy rather in the same way as people at a normal funeral would seek to comfort the widow.

Abbie, for her part was not affected in the same way as her mother whose arm she held onto during the whole proceedings and aftermath. She was not able to display any public grief for her father and she contented herself with being a support for her mother. Inside she felt a severe shock or dissatisfaction with the whole procedure which she had just observed. She thought it had all been a complete charade and that her father's suffering had not been properly delved into and she still blamed herself for not having appreciated his internal distress.

A week later Abbie and Mavis met up again at their weekly college class. During their lunch break Abbie told her all about the hearing in the coroner's court and Mavis sympathised with her and told her that she had already sent a brief to Phillipa Fry at Clifton chambers in Bristol.

"I will update her with the judgement given in the coroner's court," she said. "And let you know what she has to say about that. I don't know if she will be surprised by that. She has already let me know that she is able to see us on Thursday. Will you be able to come with me then, for a conference?"

Abbie confirmed that she would be able to go with her and they arranged to meet up early on Thursday morning at the railway station.

Accordingly, they met at the station and enjoyed chatting on the train on their way to Bristol. Inevitably, their conversation came round to the subject of Abbie's father's death.

"As promised I updated Phillipa with the result of the coroner's court hearing," she told Abbie. "She did not seem to be at all surprised by that information, I don't think she has much confidence in our local coroner's court."

"She's not the only one," said Abbie who then began a detailed description of the hearing and the coroner's judgement. Before she had finished, she had broken down in tears.

"I am so sorry," she said. " I don't want to embarrass you again with my snivelling."

"Go ahead," said Mavis. "Let it all out."

Their train pulled into Temple Meads station in Bristol and Abbie dried her eyes and they alighted from the train and made their way through the streets to Clifton chambers and announced themselves at the reception desk and were immediately shown into the room of Phillipa Fry.

What Abbie saw was a cosy well-proportioned room with an impressive bookcase well stocked with legal volumes and a large leather covered desk. She also saw a young lady (about mid-thirties), with extraordinary bright eyes, beautifully made up who jumped up from her chair and embraced Mavis as they entered the room. It was obvious from their mutual embrace, how much they cared for each other. Mavis introduced her to Phillipa.

"Please sit down," said Phillipa opening the folder on her desk. "First, I would like to say how sorry I am for your loss."

Abbie thanked her as she sat down and waited to hear what else she had to say.

"Well," she said. "I would like first of all, to congratulate Mavis for the usual high standard of her brief. You never fail to impress me, Mavis. Your briefs surpass most of the briefs I receive from all the local solicitors. I have perhaps more sympathy for you and your mother than perhaps you might expect. I recently represented a widow whose husband had attempted to take his own life. Fortunately for his family his attempt was unsuccessful but nevertheless the similarity between your two cases was uncanny. The same gaming company were involved, and I can assure you that they are a company which is beneath my contempt. The way they shamelessly prey on problem gamblers by treating them as VIP customers who are groomed with free bets and incentives to keep spending is despicable yet hugely productive from their point of view. They had no concern for the life of my previous client, and I am sure that the same attitude was displayed for your father.

"The Gambling Commission have shown little interest in investigating the deaths from suicide and having a better understanding of which products and practices of the industry cause addiction and suicide. If they had shown more interest, it might have enabled them to be a better regulator, more capable of protecting the public. The Commission, I am sorry to say has shown few teeth and I would not expect them to either investigate this matter or take any action which might impress this company to offer any compensation in respect of their appalling behaviour.

"No, this company are beyond the pale and can never be expected to offer anything unless forced to. I plan to force them into making an offer. I will send them a threat to issue a writ in the High Court. I will send a copy of the intended writ and give them short notice of the issue of said writ if they fail to comply with my demands. They will know me from the recent case which I took against them and be aware that I do not bluff so I am hoping they will concede if they know what is good for them. The writ will allege their actions were a clear and flagrant breach of their social responsibilities. I am confident that they will be eager to settle and if they do so before the time runs out, we will save considerable costs and expenses of the court proceedings. The total in the claim in my writ will marginally exceed the amount of your father's debt to this loathsome company."

Abbie was astonished and put her hands over her ears to indicate the shock which she felt.

"That is far, far, more than I could ever have dreamed would be possible. I cannot believe that. Are you confident that can be achieved?"

"Completely sure!" replied Phillipa. "I know these people and they know me. Be assured, they will fold and will not risk involving the Gambling Commission in this matter. If they do, they will be fined by the Commissioners and their costs will be doubled."

"You are so brilliant, Phillipa," said Mavis excitedly, as they rose to leave. The pair promised to stay in contact and meet up again soon.

On their return journey home on the train Abbie told Mavis how grateful she was that she had introduced her to Phillipa Fry, "You were absolutely right about her. She was amazing!"

"Isn't she so," confirmed Mavis. "And did you notice her immaculate eye make up? She really is outstanding, and she is a good friend to me. She lives with a Crown Court Judge who is handsome and just so amazing and when we got married in a special ceremony in our conservatory, they were special guests."

Abbie was more astounded by that information than the revelations which Phillipa had earlier disclosed. When they finally got back, she gave Mavis an enormous hug and kissed her.

"I cannot thank you enough Mavis. You have proved to be such a good friend."

"You are entirely welcome," responded Mavis. "It cheers me up so much to see you improving in spirits."

One more sisterly hug and then they separated.

Chapter 33

The international detective was seated in his office considering the information which he had unearthed. He was convinced that the taxi driver Phil Johnson must have been the person who had passed the fifty-pound note in the Lock & Key ironmongery shop off the town square. He had made this assumption based upon the box he had seen in his kitchen area, namely an unopened box containing a locking device for an up and over garage door.

What he did not understand was how and why Phil Johnson had done what he did and what future plans he had. Charlie had a lifetime's experience of dealing with thieves and law breakers and Phil did not compare with any of those he had met. When speaking to him he could not sense any furtiveness about the man. He seemed to be a man who was utterly normal and honest and yet he appeared to be in possession of the money and presumably must have been involved in the removal of the package from the security firm, but he did not have any scent of dishonesty about him.

Charlie tried to analyse the situation. His assessment of Phil Johnson convinced him of his general honesty and that it was virtually an impossibility that he would have been involved in the theft of the money from the security firm premises. He was left with the only remaining explanation, that Stephen Pike must have left his backpack in Phil's taxi when he went to the vaccination centre, and when he never returned, Phil had found it and discovered the cash inside it. That was entirely plausible, and Charlie was sure that would have been what happened. What he did not understand was how, having found the cash, someone as seemingly honest as Phil, could be tempted to retain the money rather than contact the police immediately.

His telephone rang and he snatched up the receiver.

"Chivers detective agency," he bellowed.

"Charlie, it's me," said Des. "Are you free for lunch in the Jubilee Inn? I have some news for you."

"Yes, absolutely," replied Charlie. "See you there in about fifteen minutes."

Charlie then scooped up his papers and his Daily Mail and put them in his battered old briefcase. He gave a hurried glance around the room to make sure he had not forgotten anything, and then, with a nod of acknowledgement to the calendar girl on the wall, exited his office and made his way downstairs. As he passed the doorway of Huw Roberts & Co he wondered about Mavis and how she was. He glanced through the glass doorway into the reception area and saw that Mavis was there at the reception talking to a lady behind the front desk. She had her coat in her hand and appeared to be on her way out. He waited outside hoping that she might appear shortly.

Sure, enough in a few minutes Mavis appeared at the doorway and greeted him.

"Hi, Charlie," she said. "How are you? What are you up to?"

Charlie told her that he was on his way to meet Des in the Jubilee Inn for another chat about information regarding the security firm robbery.

"I will update you later," he assured her.

"Oh thanks, Charlie," she said, then enthusiastically she told him quickly about how she had been on a conference with Abbie the day before at Clifton chambers with Phillipa Fry.

"She has already prepared a monster writ which she is threatening to serve on the gaming company with whom her dad had run up a huge debt. She is warning them that unless they withdraw their debt fully, she will issue the writ in the High Court and serve them up for dinner. She is so marvellous, and I am so proud of her. I know it won't bring her dad back but if she succeeds in getting the debt cancelled it will make such a difference to Abbie and her mother."

Charlie agreed that it was such good news but had to rush away to meet Des. They said their goodbyes and Charlie walked on to the Jubilee Inn. When he walked through the door, he found Reg behind the bar as usual; he greeted Charlie cheerfully. Instead of reaching for his pint glass Reg nodded towards their favourite table and Charlie was surprised to see Des sat at the table with two full pint glasses in front of him. He sat down beside him and took a long swig of the beer provided.

"Hi there," he said. "I was surprised to see you here waiting for me. I was slightly delayed leaving the office, I bumped into Mavis who had some exciting news to tell me. She went with the young trainee solicitor, Abbie, to see her favourite barrister Phillipa Fry about the death of her father and the debts he left behind him. Apparently, she is intending to bully the gaming company in the High Court to make them cancel the debts on the basis of their lack of social responsibility. I suppose if anyone can do it it's her. Mavis was cock-a-hoop."

"She's a great girl" said Des. "They've got fish and chips on the menu today. I ordered two for us."

"Great!" said Charlie. "So what news have you got for me?"

Des took a sip of his beer and smiled.

"Some more of those notes have turned up," he said.

"Really?" responded Charlie with raised eyebrows. "Where did they appear?"

"Well," said Des. "You'll never guess no matter how long you try. You can think, flashy car? Or posh hotel and holiday, or posh house. What else would you spend ill-gotten gains on?"

"I've no idea," said Charlie. "I guess I would spend most of it all on beer and young women and fritter away the rest."

"Yes, very amusing," said Des.

Just then the fish and chips arrived so all conversation was delayed for a few moments. They both tucked into their meal and relished the flavour.

"Hmm," said Des. "Absolutely delicious. Where were we? Oh yes, I know. How about medical clinics in payment for cataracts and or hip replacement operations?"

"No?" said Charlie. "You are right, I would never have guessed that. Who passed the notes, do we know?"

Des gave him the information about Beryl who had received a replacement hip, and Oswald who had received a laser operation to remove cataracts from his eyes.

"Neither of them had sufficient money to afford those operations. Both of them received an envelope which contained the money which paid for the operations together with identical anonymous well-wisher notes telling them that the doner was pleased to end their suffering by paying for their treatment. No other information was offered apart from the fact that they were each delivered at their treatment centres by taxi."

Charlie pricked up his ears at this information.

"Of course," he said with finality. "That is the answer to everything. It all makes sense at last."

He told Des about his visit to the home of Phil Johnson the taxi driver and the box he had seen containing the locking device for an up and over garage door.

"It all fits together," he said. "I assessed him as basically honest and straight forward and am certain he would not have been involved in the theft of the money. No, I am convinced that the cleaner left the backpack in his taxi, and he kept it. What I did not understand was why an honest man would need to keep the money and not inform the police of his discovery. Now I understand, it was not for himself but for the people who were suffering."

"I see," said Des. "I think I will have to have a word with him."

"Yes," said Charlie. "I think you will find that Phil Johnson has no connection with Mr Jones and I am sure that neither of them knows the other."

"I guess I will need a search warrant when I see him, to be able to look for the balance of the money before he spends any more of it?"

"I don't think he will be spending any more of it unless he already has another good cause in mind."

They both finished their fish and chips and Des declared that he had to rush because he was busy. He did say however that he would shortly be interviewing Mr Jones.

"I'm not sure how close that will bring us to discovering who planned the robbery. Or should I say, how he planned it and how we are going to prove it?"

Chapter 34

Abbie awoke early in the morning and made herself a bowl of porridge and a cup of tea. She sat on a stool and reflected on her day out with Mavis at the barristers' chambers in Bristol. She had to admit to herself that Phillipa Fry was an amazing person. Mavis had assured her of how wonderful the lady was but she herself had always been sceptical about that. However, upon meeting her she had to admit to herself that she seemed to be everything that Mavis had promised.

Yesterday evening she had explained it all to her mother who was less impressed.

"No," she had said. "Big companies like that just don't back down. You know as well as I do that they never give in ; they are too strong to be bullied. If we owed money to Tesco after dad's death they would not relent. They would insist on their pound of flesh. The money will have to be paid; we will have to sell the house to repay them. There is no other way out."

"No mum," she had told her. "It's a political thing, big companies can be persuaded that anything is advisable if it saves them money. If the Gambling Commission get to hear about this and get their teeth into it, then they would undoubtedly fine the company heavily as well as order them to discharge dad's debt. Also, it would be bad publicity for them and might well attract further applicants who might wish to sue them."

But Stephanie refused to understand what her daughter was telling her and remained convinced that she would have to sell her house. Abbie knew that she would have to wait and see what happened and realized that her own opinion wavered between the buoyant, enthusiastic attitude of Mavis, and the rigid defeatist attitude of her mother. She could see the merits of each point of view, and she knew which one she preferred to hitch her colours to.

She was reminded that today was her college day and she looked forward to seeing Mavis again. She was so enamoured with her and felt that in such a short time she had become her closest and most loving friend. She could not quantify how helpful she had been already and so loving and understanding. She also reflected upon how beautiful her house was.

Fancy finding a millionaire and marrying him she thought to herself. That reminded her of her, so far unsuccessful, internet courting which had taken a back seat since her father's death. She gave herself a memory jog to contact Joyce with a view of having a drink and a chat later today.

Stephanie came into the kitchen looking no less miserable than she had been the day before and put the kettle on for a cup of tea. She was still wearing her dressing gown and slippers which had come to be the norm for her nowadays.

"Are you going to work today?" she asked.

"Yes, of course," replied Abbie. "Well, actually I'm off to college for most of the day so I'll be seeing Mavis again today."

Stephanie frowned when she heard this which gave her daughter some idea of the attitude of her mother to the young lady who had dared to launch the possible High Court litigation which she had been discussing the day before.

"Don't let her talk you into too much," she warned pessimistically. "I do not want a large solicitors' bill on top of the enormous debt which your poor father has left behind him."

She then began a spontaneous quiet weeping which prompted Abbie to grasp her and give her a hug.

"Try not to be permanently bleak," she told her mother. "I am more optimistic than you are and still believe that there could be a brighter future. If you had seen Phillipa Fry I think you might understand where I am coming from. How long will Aunt Dorothy be staying?"

"She said she would be going home at the end of today if it's OK with me. I think that she is worried that your uncle could not last much longer on his own. It has been good to have her here, but I think that now is the natural time for her to go home."

"I thought I might give Joyce a ring and see if she might like to come round for a chat with me this evening," said Abbey. "I haven't seen her for a couple of weeks."

"Oh yes," said her mother. "Please do, I 'm sure it will be good for you."

Before she left for work, Abbie sought out Dorothy for a hug and kiss and profuse gratitude for being a sympathetic companion to her mother for a week or so. Then she left to go to work for an hour or so before moving on to the college at about mid-morning. When she arrived, she was so pleased to see Mavis again and thanked her once more for her kindness on the previous day. As they lunched together Abbie told her of her mother's melancholic attitude towards the aims and suggestions of Phillipa Fry.

"But I do not share her pessimism," she assured Mavis. "I thought Phillipa was a real marvel."

"And so she is," agreed Mavis. "Imagine your mother's improvement when she finds that all his debts are wiped out."

Abbie loved her optimism and knew that was one of the reasons she liked her so much. Before the lunchtime break was over she phoned Joyce and she agreed to call round at Abbie's house for the evening.

Accordingly, after teatime the doorbell rang, and it was Joyce. Abbie was pleased to see her after so long. Although they had spoken on the telephone, so that Joyce was aware of what had happened to her father, they had not met up for a proper chat for over two weeks.

Stephanie was quite pleased to see her as well and was content for her daughter to have her friend back. They all chatted in the kitchen-diner area for about twenty minutes until Abbie announced that they were going up to her bedroom for a chat.

Once they were up there each holding a glass of wine, Abbie got out her laptop and said to her friend, "Let's see if there have been any messages during the two weeks we have been away." She plugged in her laptop and switched it on and then scrolled down through her messages. She located a message from Pete the plumber who had answered her last message. He informed her that he would be only too pleased to rub suntan lotion into her back and would love to see her topless on his deck.

He was honest enough to admit that the boat did not belong solely to him but was shared between himself and his brother. It used to be his grandfather's boat, which is a rambling old craft, and which was left to the two grandsons on his death. Pete's brother who was slightly older, did not live in the area and was busy running a business and so that left Pete with the responsibilities for the boat. Still, he told her, "My kids love to go out on it, it's moored on the river so easy to get to and it's fun to go down to the sea on it."

"He sounds quite nice, doesn't he?" said Joyce.

"Hmm, yes," said Abbie without full enthusiasm. "I'm still not sure about the fact that he has three kids."

"I know," said Joyce. "But you have to admit he sounds nice. Ask him how old the kids are and how often he sees them?"

"OK, I will," said Abbie and began clicking away on her keyboard. "I'll also ask him what other hobbies he has."

Having sent this message, she then scrolled down the page of messages received. They both reviewed all of them but could not discern among them any of much interest.

"I guess we have to wait to see if Pete replies this evening," said Abbie. "That is always assuming that he is even using his computer this evening."

They continued chatting to each other for about half an hour, but no reply was received from Pete. Joyce then decided that it was time for her to go home and so they made their way downstairs. Stephanie was seated in the lounge watching the television. Joyce said her goodnights to both of them and then left. Abbie announced that she was going to bed and gave her mother a kiss and went upstairs to bed.

Chapter 35

Des was having an inspired day. He had already solved two crimes by using his analytical powers and another by sheer bluff and bombast with a defendant who did not know what had hit him. He had also assigned off a couple of other jobs to lower staff who were content to receive them. That left him free to concentrate on the security firm robbery.

He decided that he ought to try another interview with Mr Jones even though he knew or sensed that he was far too canny to make any admissions. He was also aware that he had little or no solid evidence to link him with the disappearance of the money. However, he thought, he had to start somewhere.

He delegated to his sergeant the job of bringing Jones into the police station for questioning. What really worried him was the likelihood that as soon as Jones realized that he was a suspect that he would refuse to answer any questions without access to a solicitor, and as soon as he obtained legal advice, he would be advised to say nothing and then the process would come to a halt. He knew that he needed some extra solid evidence or a confession from Mr Jones and he was certain that the latter would not be likely to occur.

He wondered if it might be a worthwhile exercise to apply for a search warrant for Jones' house but he knew in his heart that there was very little persuasive argument that could be included in an application for a search warrant aside from a statement that he had a strong hunch. He reviewed in his mind how he could approach an interview with the man. Should he play it quietly and softly, or should he try to bully or bluff him into submission?

I think I'll play it by ear" he thought to himself, but wished that he had Charlie alongside him for this interview. Charlie always had a certain style during an interview which he found helpful and always had the knack of asking the right question at the right time.

His sergeant came into his office to advise him that Mr Jones was on the premises and waiting in an interview room.

"How did he seem?" he asked.

The sergeant screwed up his face a little and said, "Oh, he's OK. Claims to be happy to help in any way possible, but I'm not sure I believe him."

"No, nor do I," said Des. "Anyway, let's go in and see what he's got to say for himself."

The sergeant followed him down to the interview room and they both entered and sat down.

"Good morning, Mr Jones. I am DCI O'Nighons. Thank you for coming in to talk to us. I am bound to advise you that you are entitled to have a solicitor present should you want one. Do you wish to call one?"

Jones pretended to look surprised.

"Should I?" he asked. "I thought I was just here to help you with some information?"

"Precisely," said Des. "I wasn't suggesting that you should have one, I was merely advising you of your rights. If you don't feel that you need one, then we will proceed." He switched on the tape machine, detailed the time and date and the names of those present.

"So, what can you tell us about the disappearance of the cash from your security firm?"

"Well," he said suavely. "Nothing more than I've already told you. You have seen the CCTV video from the garage, you've seen the cleaner leaving the premises with the ill-gotten gains. Shouldn't you be following that up, perhaps searching his house to find out what he did with the money?"

"The CCTV tape does not prove that he took the money," said Des. "It only shows him leaving the premises wearing a backpack."

"Precisely," said Jones as if Des was a complete idiot. "His backpack full of fifty-pound notes. No one else had the access or the opportunity. What I don't understand is why you people aren't looking for it. It must have been him, but where did he leave the backpack? That is the question which you people must answer. He must have either left it behind in his house or taken it with him to the vaccination centre. Why aren't you out there looking for it instead of wasting your time talking to me here?"

"Well," said Des. "He could have passed it to anyone after he left your premises, couldn't he? For example, he could have passed it to you on the road outside the security firm, or to anybody he knew or met when he arrived at the vaccination centre. We must explore all possibilities and ask any relevant questions. For example, can you please tell us how well you knew Stephen Pike?"

"Hardly at all," he said, then rather grandly. "He was a reasonably good cleaner I believe; I would see him from time to time, but I was always too busy to stop and talk to him."

"So," said Des casually. "You never had any social contact with him outside of work?"

"Good heavens no," said Jones arrogantly. "I was management, he was a cleaner!"

Des smiled inwardly but delayed playing his ace card. First, he asked a final question.

"So," he said, seemingly unconcerned. "You would never have gone fishing with him?"

Mr Jones looked flabbergasted and said, "No, of course not."

Des shuffled his papers and slid across the table the photograph which Charlie had passed to him which showed Jones with his arm around a smiling Stephen Pike proudly holding a freshly caught fish.

"So how do you explain this Mr Jones?" he asked. "Do you do a lot of fishing?"

Jones stared at the picture for a few seconds and his countenance stiffened.

"That's not me," he said. "It looks a bit like me, but it is not me. I have never been a fisherman."

Des gave a glance to his sergeant and pulled an incredulous face and also gave a snort of disbelief.

"I think the time has come for me to revert to a more formal legal position," said Jones adopting a thin upper lipped attitude. "I did try to help you but find that you are not interested in searching for the truth. I do not wish to say anything more to you until I have spoken to a solicitor."

Des ended the interview formally and switched off the machine.

"Do you have a solicitor whom you wish to contact? If not, one can be provided from the rota."

Chapter 36

Abbigail was up at the crack of dawn on the day of her next attendance day at college. She always liked to get to work extra early to make up for the time later in the day when she was not in the office. She had made herself some cereal with blueberries and a cup of green tea which she was just tucking into when her mother walked into the kitchen. As usual she was wearing her dressing gown and slippers.

Stephanie looked bleary eyed and worn.

"I'm going to put the property on the market today and have a look round to see what we will be able to afford to buy in its place."

"Oh no mother," cried Abbie despairingly. "Not yet just wait until we hear from Phillipa Fry. Don't give up until she tells us to."

"No," said her mother decisively. "It does not pay to hold on for possible fairy tale endings. It makes more sense to be realistic and make plans while we have plenty of time, not leave it until the bailiffs are knocking on the door. I think the new property should be put into our joint names."

"That is a good idea mum but please hang on for another week or so to find out what success Phillipa may achieve."

Stephanie was not convinced and told Abbie that she had decided to contact the estate agent today who would no doubt call round to value the property.

"By the time you get home from work I will be able to tell you how much the property is worth."

Abbie did not have any more time to argue the point. She told her mother that she was going to work and that they might be able to talk about it when she got home. She left the house and made her way to work and settled down for a couple of hours of work before leaving to go to the college. When she got there she sat next to Mavis whom she was thrilled to see but there was no time for a chat because the teacher was early. The first time they actually spoke to each other therefore was at lunchtime.

They ordered their snack and coffee and sat down at a table. Mavis had a face like a spring morning. She said to Abbie.

"I have something to show you," she said with barely concealed excitement.

She produced a message page which she brandished triumphantly and spread it out on the table.

"It's from Phillipa Fry," she said, her eyes glowing like fire coals.

"They've completely folded! They have signed a full admission and wiped out the entire debt. Isn't that wonderful?"

Abbie stared at the document for a moment and then her eyes welled up and she wrapped her arms around Mavis and whispered in her ear, "Mavis, you are so marvellous, thank you so very much."

Mavis gave a laugh of sheer joy and said, "You are so very welcome."

Chapter 37

Phil Johnson awoke on a grey morning which reflected and mirrored his own mood and condition. He felt throughout his whole body a numbing pain which persisted even when he was lying in his bed. With great pain and difficulty, he got out of bed and gradually got dressed. For the first time in his life, he experienced what it was like to get dressed by instalments. After each item donned, he had to rest and breathe deeply and plan carefully the next action which he would take. He found that his socks were the most difficult items. He realized that some poor people never knew what it was like to not experience such daily pain and inconvenience. He wondered how Beryl was now, one week on from her operation. He guessed that she should be home by now and he thought that he would like to go round to see her, to witness for himself her personal improvement before transferring himself to the wellness clinic.

He hobbled into the kitchen and plundered one of the cupboards for a packet of painkillers which he opened. He pressed two tablets out of the aluminium sheet and poured himself some water to swallow them down. He had lately purchased many packets in order to give himself some regular relief from the encroaching ubiquitous pain.

He walked outside and opened his car door and extracted the windscreen wiper from the driver's door panel. He scraped his windscreen clear of frost and then eased himself painfully into the driving seat. He started the engine and sat in the car for a few minutes allowing the car to warm up. Eventually, he put the car in gear and drove round to Beryl's house. He parked outside and rang her doorbell. It took a long time for the door to be answered but Phil was expecting Beryl to take time walking to the door. When the door was finally opened Beryl was stood inside with a metal walking frame. When she saw Phil, her face lit up and she summoned him into her kitchen and insisted on making a pot of coffee.

He sat himself down at her kitchen table.

"So," he said. "How are you feeling, Beryl?"

"I am so well, thanks to you," she said. "I still have to use this (she indicated the walking frame), because walking around will take about a month they say, but I now feel no pain. I have not felt this well for many years and it's all thanks to you."

She served the coffees and sat down opposite him and examined his face properly for the first time since she had opened the door. She observed the greyness of his face, the pale watery patina of his skin, and the generally tired expression.

"My god, Phil, you look terrible, what has happened to you?"

He gave an indifferent wince and waved a hand as if to banish any of life's problems but informed her about his cancer which had now taken hold of his body with an iron grip.

"I thought I had mentioned it before," he assured her. "It has been around for several years. It started in the prostate but because there were no symptoms it was allowed to fester away inside me without being discovered. Now it has moved on to the rest of my body and is completely incurable. They have estimated that I have no more than one month left and will be moving into the End-of-Life clinic which is situated in the former railway station near the floral park. I have told my daughter and son are aware of the situation. I am sorry to say that I will no longer be able to drive you to Tesco's."

"Oh, I am so sorry, Phil. How ironic that you should have done so much for me while you were so ill. Don't worry about my journey to Tesco, I will soon be able to walk there soon. In fact, I will soon be walking everywhere. But what about you?"

Once again, Phil gave an expression of indifference and swatted the air with his hand as if to dismiss the concern, with a pale sickly imperviousness.

"It's too late, Beryl," he said. "It's a matter of days."

He sipped the coffee which she had given him but could not finish it. He got to his feet and made his way along her hallway and turned in the doorway to say his goodbye. Beryl realized then that he had come to her house to say his final goodbye. She welled up and threw herself into his arms and wept quietly as he struggled to hold her up.

"Goodbye Phil and thanks for everything," she said.

Phil stepped away and the difficulty which he clearly had in taking the few steps to his car recalled for her the constant pain and discomfort which accompanied every step that she had previously taken. She watched as he drove away and wiped a tear from her eye.

Phil, as he drove, determined that he would make his way home and pack his bag and travel this day to the clinic which Mr Khan had assured him had a vacant room ready and waiting for him. He made a quick inventory of the things he would need. Few clothes, he thought, just fling a few items into a bag or case, take his phone remembering to take also his re-charging device, and toothbrush and tooth paste and perhaps a toilet roll or two. He thought also that he would need to take with him the spare key to his own house to be able to hand it over to his son and/or daughter when they came to visit him. He also thought that a pen and paper might be useful to enable him to make notes about anything which he may wish to bring to the attention of his son or daughter. He realized that although this situation had been creeping up on him for many months, he was still ill-equipped to deal with it. He thought to himself that he had not been inside a church for so many years and had no thoughts for any hymns or words to be said on his behalf at a funeral. He also wondered, in the present Covid situation, how many people would be allowed to attend. On the other hand, he realized that in any event there would be very few mourners anyway.

Chapter 38

Abbie arrived home from work to find her mother in the kitchen filling up cardboard boxes with some of the contents of the kitchen cupboards.

"What are you doing?" she said.

Her mother pointed to an estate agent's particulars lying on the work top. The document was open at the page which gave advice to a prospective seller by suggesting that the most important room in the house was the kitchen. The volume reminded sellers that the kitchen was the first room in the house that should receive attention.

"Mother, I repeat, what are you doing?"

Stephanie looked up and then indicated the particulars again and said, "I'm doing what they suggest, I'm minimalizing the kitchen area which is the most important part as far as a buyer is concerned."

"Mother!" said Abbie again. "Listen to me for a moment, just sit down and listen while I tell you. You don't need to do any of this, just listen while I tell you."

She got hold of her mother by the arm and led her to a stool and made sure she was seated. She pulled out the copy paper which Mavis had given to her.

"Look at this, Mum," she said showing the paper to her. "This is confirmation from Phillipa Fry that the gaming company have completely folded and wiped out all dad's debt and admitted they were at least partly to blame. You don't have to sell the house mum, it's all yours with no outstanding debt. Do you understand mum?"

Stephanie looked blankly at her daughter and looked shell-shocked.

"Really?" she said almost disbelieving. "No more debt? Are you sure?"

"Absolutely," confirmed Abbie. "It's all in writing, no more debt."

Stephanie drew breath and waited a second then said again.

"No more debt?" she asked again.

"No more debt," confirmed Abbie once more.

Stephanie stayed rigid for a moment and then eventually she began to cry. Abbie hugged her and patted her shoulders as her mother wept with tears of relief. Eventually she stopped crying and Abbie switched on the kettle for a cup of tea, but Stephanie took control and said, "This calls for a proper drink, let's have a gin and tonic and celebrate."

Abbie agreed with her so that is what they did.

"I have asked Joyce to come round again this evening," said Abbie.

Stephanie nodded and smiled at her daughter and said, "That'll be nice for you."

Later Joyce arrived and joined Abbey and her mother briefly in their lounge where Abbie announced to her the good news about the capitulation of the gaming company and the huge sense of relief felt by both herself and her mother.

"That is really good news," agreed Joyce. "I can understand how relieved you both must feel."

"Yes," said Abbey with a big triumphal smile. "Mum and I have already had a drink to celebrate, but now you are here I think we should have another. Do you agree, Mum?"

Stephanie nodded and smiled too.

"You know where the gin is, Abbey."

Abbie went out of the room and soon returned with three glasses of gin and tonic. They all sat together for a few minutes while Abbey told Joyce all about the legal process which had been choreographed by the wonderful Phillipa Fry.

"She was brilliant," she told Joyce. "Mum was ready to sell the house. It was the only way to clear the debt until She stepped in and forced the gaming company to write off the debt in its entirety. Such a relief!"

Joyce could see and understand what it meant to Abbey and her mother and told them she was very happy for them. Abbey then announced that she and Joyce were going up to her bedroom for a gossip. Once they were up in her bedroom Abbie got out her laptop and switched it on.

"Let's have a look and see if there have been any messages from Pete the plumber," she said fingering the keyboard and scanning the menu on the screen.

"Aah," she said. "Here we are."

Joyce sat beside her, and they both looked at the message received from Pete the plumber.

"So," read Abbie. "He's got three children all girls, the eldest is nine years old, and the other two are twins aged seven years old. He says they are all three taking dancing lessons and will be taking part in a Christmas concert at the local playhouse. He sees them every fortnight and whenever the sun is out, he takes them out on his boat which they all three are madly in love with, and so is he with them."

"Oh," declared Joyce. "He sounds so lovely, doesn't he?"

"He says he also likes sports of all kind, he plays tennis and goes swimming, and he also plays guitar and plays in a band sometimes. He wants to know when we can meet up."

"Wow," said Joyce with real surprise. "He just gets better and better."

"Hmm," said Abbey who was already half convinced. "But three children, I wasn't looking for that."

"Oh, I don't know," said Joyce. "They sound like fun. I'm sure you would get on with them well or, you could just see him on the alternative weekends when he is alone. See how you get on. If you really hit it off, he might invite you to meet his girls. How romantic."

"Hmm," said Abbey. "I might give it a try but nothing serious to start with."

"That's the spirit," said Joyce. "Go on then, send him a message to say you would be willing to meet and see what he says." Abbey thought for a moment.

"OK," she said. "I will."

Chapter 39

The international detective sat at his desk and pondered over the evidence which he had already discovered. He wondered what his next step should be and who he ought to speak to. As he was considering these things the telephone on his desk rang and he snatched up the receiver and barked into the mouthpiece, "Chivers' detective agency."

"Charlie it's me," said Des. "I've got some more news for you if we can meet up in the Jubilee soon?"

"Yeah, sure," replied Charlie. "Shall we say fifteen minutes?"

"Okey dokey," confirmed Des. "I'm on my way now."

Charlie made his way down the stairs and when he got to the ground floor, he peered through the glass doorway of Hugh Roberts & Co to see if Mavis was in the reception area. Just as he looked in he saw her come out of the office corridor into the reception area. He caught her eye and waved to her, and she came over towards him and opened the door.

"Hi, Charlie," she said. "Everything all right with you?"

"Yeah, just passing on my way to meet Des," he said. "I just wondered how the matter of the debt of Abbie's dad went?"

"Oh yes," she said with great excitement. "The gaming company folded completely and the whole debt was wiped out. Phillipa Fry won the day hands down. She was brilliant as usual. I am so happy for Abbie and her mother."

"That is great news," said Charlie. "Well done to you too. Without you they would still be burdened with the debt. I must go now to meet Des but will speak to you later."

Charlie continued on his way to the Jubilee Inn. He entered the building which was empty except for the landlord Reg who was wiping the bar top with a dishcloth.

"Hello, Charlie," he said, depositing the dishcloth on one side to enable him to pick up a pint glass. He began to draw a pint of Charlie's favourite beer.

"Will Des be joining you?" he asked. Charlie nodded and so Reg drew a pint of beer for Des.

Charlie appraised the photographs on the wall behind Reg to determine if there were any new pictures offered, but he could not see any photographs which he had not seen before.

"What's on the lunch time menu today, Reg?" he asked.

"Cottage pie today, Charlie," said Reg. "Did you want some?"

"Yeah OK, better make that two, Reg," he said handing over some cash to the landlord. After pocketing the change which Reg gave him, he moved over to the table where he took a seat and extracted the Daily Mail from his battered briefcase. After about ten minutes Des arrived and joined him at the table.

"Hi," he said settling himself down on a chair and taking a gulp from his pint glass.

The lunch then arrived from the kitchen; hand delivered by Mrs Partridge straight from the kitchen.

Charlie tucked into his first spoonful of cottage pie and forkful of chips.

"How did your interview with Mr Jones go?"

"Well," said Des taking a sip of his beer. "He was very helpful, co-operation personified until I asked him if he knew the cleaner, Stephen Pike very well. He said he did not know him at all. As he put it himself, 'I am management, he was a cleaner'. He is a real snob, but despite that I suggested that he might have had some social contact with him, for example gone fishing with him. He completely pooh-poohed that notion and said never. Then, I showed the photograph of him and Stephen Pike in fishing gear holding the prize fish and asked him how he could explain it. He then adopted a frozen veneer, denied that it was him in the picture, and refused to answer any further questions without a lawyer being present."

"Wow," said Charlie. "That sounds like the next best thing to a signed confession."

"Yeah," agreed Des. "He's obviously, guilty of something. The trouble is, so far there is very little evidence to link him to anything."

"Well," said Des. "I was thinking of paying a visit to the patients who are presumably still recovering from their operations. Do you fancy coming along and listening in to what they have to say?"

Charlie said that he would and so when they had finished their lunch, they exited the Jubilee Inn with farewell calls to Reg, and made their way to Des' car, and off to meet up with Beryl and Oswald. When they knocked on Beryl's door she could only be described as shocked. She led them inside and gave them a seat in the kitchen. She listened with much anxiety to the explanation Des gave her concerning the robbery of money from the security firm and the fact that the money she had handed over for her operation had been traced and confirmed as being part of the missing money.

"Now, Beryl," he said gently. "I know you told our uniform branch that the money for your operation was delivered to your doorstep with a note which you gave to the police officers who spoke to you and a copy of which I have here," (he brandished the copy note). "Would you mind telling us who gave you the money?"

Beryl looked cornered and flummoxed, and coughed delicately.

"The note was not signed she said. I don't want to get anyone into trouble," she said awkwardly.

"I realize that," said Des. "But you see Beryl, we have to get to the bottom of this in order to track down the balance of the money which was stolen. No one is suggesting for a minute that you were involved in the robbery but by paying for your operation with some of the money you put yourself in the frame for a charge of having some vague connection with the offence. I would hate that to happen to you. Are you saying that you found it on your doorstep with the anonymous note?"

Beryl looked shell-shocked and tremored, she remembered what Phil had told her and did not want to give him away. "Eh, yes," she said cautiously and then she repeated that she did not want to get anyone into trouble.

"I understand that," he said. "And I'll tell you what I will do. I believe you were delivered to the clinic by taxi?"

Beryl nodded nervously.

"Well," said Des diplomatically. "I would like you to tell me who the taxi driver was and then I can go and have a word with him and if he tells me what I think he might tell me, I probably won't need to visit you again. Now, surely you can remember who drove you to the clinic?"

Beryl nodded dumbly. "His name is Phil Johnson," she said.

"Aah, yes," said Des. "I think we know him, don't we?" Here he glanced at Charlie briefly who did not change his expression.

"Yes," continued Des. "He lives I think next to the Methodist Hall, doesn't he?"

"Yes," agreed Beryl. "But you won't find him there now. He is in the final stages of cancer and has gone into the end-of-life clinic. I believe he only has about one week to go."

Des and Charlie excused themselves with the proviso that they might return.

Outside, Des said to Charlie, "Well, there is now no doubt about who had the money and may still have the balance. I don't think we need to bother with Oswald, let's go straight off to Phil Johnson before it's no too late."

"Yes," confirmed Charlie. "It all makes sense now that we know where he is."

Des drove them to the clinic in ten minutes. When they arrived they were both surprised at how easy it was to gain entry to Phil's room. No one asked who they were or imposed any condition upon the time that they would spend with him. Everyone simply assumed that they were close friends who had come to console him.

What struck them both, and Charlie in particular, (having recently seen Phil), was how spectre-like and close to death he looked. His skin looked like thousand-year-old parchment and his face wore a vacant, disinterested expression.

Des introduced themselves to him and he recognised Charlie and knew of course the subject matter of their visit. Des emphasised this by saying, "You no doubt know why we have come to see you." Phil nodded.

"Our enquiries showed that the money which paid for the operations for your fares Beryl and Oswald was part of the proceeds of a robbery from a local security firm."

Phil nodded and said, "There was also one of the notes which I used to buy something in town to test out whether or not you would trace the notes."

"The garage door locking device which I saw in your kitchen," said Charlie.

Phil nodded again. "I spent no other money, Beryl and Oswald had no idea where the money came from. They were suffering lots of pain and discomfort so why not assist them? Who can judge? The rest of the money is still intact and is in the backpack in the corner of the room over there."

He pointed to a corner of the room where the backpack lay.

"It's up to you what you found inside it. I won't be able to help you much longer. I'm a bit tired now."

As they both watched him, he slid away from them and was asleep in seconds. Neither of them knew if he would wake up again if ever. They decided to leave and walked out of the clinic and sat in Des' car for a few minutes.

"Well," said Des rummaging through the contents of the backpack. "This is certainly the property of Stephen Pike."

He pulled out a fishing magazine which had clearly been posted to 'Mr S. Pike' and had his address on it. He also pulled out the packet of money which he counted roughly.

"Yeah," he said. "By a rough calculation I can see that what he said was true. The whole balance is here; apart from the two operations and the garage door locking device Phil has kept none of it aside from the change from the ironmongery shop from the single fifty-pound note."

"Hmm," murmured Charlie thoughtfully. "This will require some in-depth thought on our part. Bearing in mind the fact that Phil will not be with us long enough to be expected to make a formal statement, and Stephen Pike is already deceased, there is no solid evidence of anything."

Des nodded carefully.

"We'd better get this cash back to the station while we decide exactly how we are going to describe how we came by it."

Chapter 40

When Abbie arose and went down to the kitchen to have breakfast, she was surprised to find her mother already there. She was also fully dressed in gym top and jogging bottoms and white trainers.

"Do you fancy some scrambled egg?" she asked. "Coffee is already warming up."

"Wow," said Abbie with genuine surprise. "It's good to see you up and full of beans, yes all right scrambled eggs sound lovely. Don't tell me you are intending to go to the gym today? How long is it since you last went there?"

"Oh, many months," replied Stephanie. "But I was thinking yesterday that I paid out all that membership fee so I might just as well take advantage of it."

Abbie threw her arms around her and gave her a big hug. Stephanie looked shocked and said, "What brought this on?"

Abbie just smiled and said, "Welcome back, Mum. Now where are my scrambled eggs?"

They both sat together and enjoyed their breakfast, after which Abbie gathered up her handbag and raincoat and gave her mother a goodbye kiss and went off to work. She was early today because it was a day for her college class, and she always liked to do some work extra early to make up for the time she would be out of the office. She achieved a good quiet hour's work before anyone else arrived. Mr Morris was the next in time to arrive. He looked into her room to say hello and reminded her that she was not obliged to attend early in the morning on her college day. His words were wasted on Abbie who was naturally conscientious, and he knew it.

She told him about the result of Phillipa Fry's intervention into her dad's tragic affairs which she had already told him about. He had known what was happening but had not heard the result.

"She, (Phillipa Fry), was brilliant," she assured him. "She forced them to retract the whole of dad's debt, and pay all her costs too. My mum does not have to sell the house to pay off his debts. She is a new woman who is so much more cheerful now. It is about the best possible outcome to a tragic event.

Mr Morris told her he was very happy for both her and her mother and agreed that the outcome, engineered by Phillipa Fry was as good as it could have been.

Shortly after, Abbie left the office to take the journey to the college where she would take her lesson and meet Mavis. The latter was there before her today and so they had the slight luxury of a chat before the lesson began.

"Once again," said Abbie. "I do not know how to thank you for organising the meeting with Phillipa Fry and the magnificent result which she produced. You have no idea what a difference it has made to my mother. She is a changed woman; when I left her this morning she was planning to go to the gym. She has not done that for nearly a year. It is all thanks to you and Phillipa Fry."

"You are more than welcome," replied Mavis. "It was all due to Phillipa Fry, she is the heroine not me."

"Oh, you are too modest," insisted Abbie. "I know that none of this success would have been achieved without you and I bless you for being an absolutely wonderful friend."

The tutor then arrived, and the lesson began and continued until the lunchtime break. Mavis and Abbie then repaired to the coffee/snack bar which was their favourite venue.

"That private detective you put me in touch with is brilliant," said Abbie.

"Oh, Charlie," said Mavis. "Yes, he is good isn't he. He was in the CID for about twenty years. He also has connections with the local CID with whom he shares information."

"Yes, he told me a bit about that," said Abbie. "I think he is planning to report to me soon. He lets me know about once a week on his progress and I am enormously impressed with him and am grateful for your recommendation."

"Oh, no problem," said Mavis. "So how is the rest of your life doing? Are you getting over the sad news about your father?"

"Yes," she said taking a huge breath. "In some ways it is something I guess I will never get over, but on a lighter note I can tell you that I have got my first date from the site I signed up to recently. A guy named Pete who has his own boat apparently. Mind you, he also has three children so I'm not sure how successful it will be."

"Wow," said Mavis excitedly. "That is lovely. I do hope it all goes well for you."

"Oh, so do I," said Abbie. "I must admit that I am quite excited about it. He looks and seems a really nice chap which is very encouraging but, he has so many responsibilities, he runs his own business, and has three children, all girls, one is nine years old and the other two are twins who are seven years old. He sounds like a good father which is quite cute. All the same I wonder if I'm ready to dip my toe into water that deep."

"Hmm," said Mavis nodding her head. "I know where you are coming from, but why not give it a try and see how you feel. You're not committed to anything; just have a look and see what you think. I expect it will be just as nerve wracking for him."

"Yes, of course," said Abbie. "You are so wise Mavis."

They both laughed heartily.

Chapter 41

Des was back inside the police station, considering the information which he and Charlie had discovered in their travels. He had pondered on what to do with the cash which had been in the backpack formerly belonging to Stephen Pike. His two options were to either deposit the cash in the police bank account and settle up with the security firm (or their insurers), or to simply return the cash to the security firm direct. After some consideration he decided to go with the first alternative and keep the money in the bank account of the police authority. In either event he realized that he would have to advise the security firm of the discovery of the cash and buy sufficient time for himself when deciding precisely what information would go into the report that he would eventually prepare.

Having made this decision, he decided also to visit the security firm straight away to appraise them of the information he had unearthed. He also hoped to see Mr Jones and maybe interview him again. He picked up his phone and asked for his sergeant to step into his office. A few seconds later the sergeant stepped into his room and Des explained to him that they would both be visiting the security firm to inform them of the fact that most of the stolen money had been recovered. He had already told his sergeant about the recovery of the money and had also instructed him to pay the cash into the police bank account. The sergeant assured him that the money had been deposited in the bank already.

"Well, that's good I guess," replied Des. "No doubt they will ask us to return the recovered money to them straight away, but I think it is better if it stays where it is for now. They will have to wait until our investigations have been completed. Which reminds me, I think we ought to make a further interview with our friend Mr Jones a priority today."

The sergeant agreed and said he had already made an application and obtained a search warrant for the security firm premises in readiness for further investigations which included further interview(s), with Mr Jones.

"Right," said Des, getting to his feet. "Let's get on with it and see what we can find out."

They left the office and made their way to the station car park and took Des' car which he drove to the security firm building. They both marched into the reception area on the ground floor and spoke to the receptionist. Des showed her his identity card and asked to speak with Mr Jones. The receptionist told him that Mr Jones was not in the building today and suggested that he might wish to call another day instead. Des informed her that the matter was too important to allow delay and asked who else was available for him to speak to.

"Well," she said. "The manager Mr Wilkinson has just returned from our head office today. Shall I ask him if he can see you?"

"Des said that was a good idea and if he had known that the manager was back he would have asked to see him, anyway."

He and the sergeant waited in the reception waiting area until they were shown into the office of the manager Mr Wilkinson. This gentleman was clearly close to retirement. He had a full head of hair which was silvery white in colour. Surprisingly, his eyebrows had remained dark, almost black in colour, and even more surprisingly he boasted a bushy moustache which was a shade of light ginger.

"Thank you for seeing us," said Des. "I was hoping to see Mr Jones."

"He is not here today," said Mr Wilkinson. "But I presume that your visit here today concerns the money which was stolen from here?"

Des nodded and said, "Yes, that is correct. We did speak to Mr Jones recently and we were hoping to ask him a few more questions today. When will he next be available?"

Mr Wilkinson shook his head, frowned and said.

"I am not absolutely sure," he said. "He did not come into work today and we have presumed that he must be unwell but have received no confirmation yet."

Des looked very concerned and asked, "So, has anyone spoken to him today?"

"No, not so far as I am aware," he replied. "I have been away for just over two weeks and only returned today. As it is Monday today, I assume that the last time anyone saw Mr Jones here was last Friday."

"Can you check with someone to confirm that please?" said Des.

Mr Wilkinson picked up his phone and spoke to someone for a short while. He put down the phone and spoke to Des, "Yes, he was here last Friday although apparently he left at lunchtime and no one has seen or heard from him since. Everyone has assumed, I think, that he was unwell and would be returning as soon as he recovers."

"Hmm," said Des with a critical air. "I will have to look into this more fully and make further enquiries. I can tell you that we have found the majority of the money which has been deposited in the police bank account and a full report will be made shortly for you and your insurance company. In the meantime, I have lots to do and will speak to you later. Can you please let me have the private address of Mr Jones?"

Mr Wilkinson checked a file on his computer and wrote down on a slip of paper the address of Mr Jones and passed it across the desk. Des picked up the piece of paper and read it, nodding to himself. He stood up and said, "Well, thank you Mr Wilkinson, I will be in touch with you soon." He handed over his personal card and said, "If Mr Jones returns or gets in touch with you please contact me immediately on this number."

Mr Wilkinson nodded dumbly and wondered what exactly was going on as he watched Des and his sergeant leaving the room.

Des drove himself and his sergeant back to the station. Once he was back in his own room Des delegated to his sergeant the task of checking all aeroplane flights out of the UK during the previous seventy-two hours. He had no definite information to persuade him that Mr Jones had attempted to flee the country, but he had a nagging feeling deep inside that that was indeed what had happened. He picked up his phone and dialled the number of the international detective.

"Chiver's detective agency!"

"Hi Charlie, it's me," he said. "I'm at the station, I've just been round to the security firm and guess what? It is looking likely that Jones has done a runner. I'm getting my boys to check aeroplane flights but while they are doing that, I thought I would check at his house in case he was still at home. Do you want to come with me?"

Charlie said he would so Des said he would pick him up in ten minutes outside his office. The detective agreed and picked up his battered brief case and his raincoat. A few minutes later Charlie was waiting in the street outside his office and Des pulled up in his car and opened his passenger door for Charlie to jump in. On his way to the house of Jones Des described to him what had happened at the security firm offices.

"So," said Charlie with some cynicism. "You reckon Jones may have done a bunk?"

"Quite frankly, I do," said Des. "Of course, he could be at home in his bed with a head cold but I can't help feeling that he got the jitters as soon as I showed him that photograph of him and Stephen Pike with the fish."

When they arrived at the road where Mr Jones resided they found a long hillside cul-de-sac full of middle-class bungalows each with a driveway and a garage. Des parked outside the right bungalow and they got out of the car and walked up the driveway. Des rang the doorbell and they waited. No one answered the door and there was no car parked in the driveway. They both looked around and Charlie saw the curtain twitch in the window of a bungalow across the road. He wandered across the road and knocked on the door which was answered by a middle-aged woman with greying hair and wire glasses.

"Good day mam, how are you? We were hoping to see Mr Jones the man who lives in the bungalow across the road (he pointed across the road), you may have noticed us knocking on the door. Do you know anything about him?"

"Yes, indeed I do," said the lady. "My husband and I own the house and can advise you of anything you need to know but first you will have to tell us who you are?"

Charlie immediately gave Des a wave, beckoning him to cross the road.

"We are a police investigation team. My name is Chivers, and this gentleman is Detective Chief Inspector O' Nighons."

As Charlie finished saying this Des arrived at her doorstep and brandished his identity card in front of her saying, "May we please come in and talk to you for a while?"

The lady led them in and took them into the lounge where a gentleman was seated in an armchair. Des and Charlie sat on the sofa and the lady sat down on the other chair.

"This is my husband," she said, the man nodded to them. "We own the bungalow across the road which formerly belonged to my parents. We have been renting it to a man called Jones for a month or two but a couple of days ago we saw him loading up possessions into his car and driving away. He owes us a month's rent, but we fear that he has gone."

"So," said Des. "Exactly how long has he been your tenant? Did he live alone or was he e.g. a married man with children or whatever?"

"No," she said. "He lived alone. He has been our tenant now for two months. He told us he had sold his house which was only a couple of miles away, and that he was planning to move abroad."

"So how did you come into contact with him?" asked Charlie.

"Through the estate agents in the high street," she answered. "I believe they sold his house for him, and we were on their books to rent our property out."

"And just to be certain, he gave you no notice or indication of his intention to leave?"

"That is right," she said. "He loaded up that Mercedes car of his and made off. He had plenty of time and opportunity to either knock on the door or leave a note. He knew what he was doing."

"OK," said Des getting to his feet. "Well, I think we will leave it there. We will go and see what the estate agents know. If you think of anything else, then please give me a ring." He handed her a card and shook the hand of her husband and then he and Charlie left the property and drove towards the estate agents' office.

When they got there, they found a small office manned by just two people, one a glamourous female wearing lots of foundation make-up, and the other a very young man in a smart blue suit. Des took the lead as usual and introduced themselves and explained what they were looking for. The made-up lady explained that their Mr Benstead was the person who had dealt with Mr Jones but that gentleman was out of the office on a job, but she would endeavour to help them.

Des told her that he needed to know everything they knew about Mr Jones.

"Perhaps you could tell me the first matter in which you acted for him. Was it when he purchased the property that he recently sold and if so, how long ago was that?"

The lady confirmed that they had acted upon the sale of the property to Mr Jones when he had bought the house about ten years ago. She was unable to recall the price he paid for the property but she did know the amount he received for it when he sold it just over two months ago. Des made a note of the sum in his notebook.

"And then, I believe, he rented the property where he lived until the other day, from Mr and Mrs eh," here he looked up the name of the couple in his notebook. "Through yourselves."

The lady nodded and confirmed that he had signed a lease through them.

"Well," said Des with some irony. "I can advise you that Mr Jones has left that property owing one month's rent. He left two days ago in a hurry. Can you tell me please which firm of solicitors acted for him on the sale of his house?"

"Certainly," she said checking her file. "It was the firm of Huw Roberts & Co."

Neither Des nor Charlie needed to write that down in a notebook. They knew that was the firm in which Mavis worked.

Chapter 42

Mavis awoke early and left George asleep in bed. She showered and dressed and went downstairs to the kitchen diner area where she made herself a bowl of cereal with some blueberries added. She found some orange juice in the fridge and poured herself a large glassful and sat down on a stool to enjoy her breakfast. As she was munching her cereal she reflected on the most recent episode in her personal and professional life namely the matter of the former debt of Abbie's father. She was so gratified with the outcome of that case not just because of the positive result achieved but also because she had been able to see her friend Phillipa Fry whom she adored.

She knew also that her intervention had given Abbie and more particularly, her mother, a huge psychological boost. She was aware that although the loss of Abbie's father was a dreadful occurrence, the sense of relief which Phillipa's action had afforded was so heartening for all concerned, including herself. As she thought about it a tear of joy rolled down her cheek. As she wiped it away George strolled into the kitchen dressed only in a pair of black boxer shorts, wiping the sleep from his eyes.

He walked behind her and wrapped his arms around her and kissed her neck.

"Hello, my darling," she said. "What are you planning to do today?"

"I am going to attack the final bedroom today," he said with assurance. "I'll start with the ceiling which I will fill and paint, and while I'm waiting for that to dry, I thought I would wash and clean the tiled floor in the conservatory. When that is finished, I will start papering the walls."

George had been gradually decorating the whole house for the last three months. He had not taken on this task through necessity, since he could easily have employed a professional firm to re-furbish the whole house. It was something he preferred to do, and he thoroughly enjoyed it.

"And have you thought about what you would like to do when you have finished this mammoth job my love," asked Mavis finishing her last mouthful of cereal.

George began to prepare a pot of coffee which would supply him with enough caffein for his morning's requirement.

"I have been thinking about that for a number of days," he said. "But I have not yet come up with an answer."

"Well, so far you have made a beautiful job of what you have done my darling. You have surprised me with your expertise. I am certain that whatever you decide upon, you will carry it out with the same skill and enthusiasm. Anyway, I am off to work now, and will see you later."

She kissed him and then left the kitchen and walked out of the front door and walked to the office where she worked. As usual she was the first to arrive and she went to her office and began working on her files. Gradually the rest of the staff arrived and Mr Ferguson the boss, when he arrived, looked into her office to see how she was getting on.

"Bright and early as ever," he commented. "You are an example to all of us, Mavis."

Mavis smiled modestly and said, "Not really, it's simply a joy to arrive early and to be able to revel in the silence and solitude."

"That matter you took on for the young lady in our rival's office worked out well I understand?"

"Yes, Abbigail," she replied. "It was so gratifying to be able to help her in such tragic circumstances. But really all credit must go to Phillipa Fry who, as always, was quite magnificent."

"Well," said Mr Ferguson. "I'm sure your modesty does you credit, but someone once said I believe that a barrister is only as good as the brief which is delivered to him."

Mavis shrugged in a self-deprecatory manner, "Well, I'm not sure about that. I gave her all the facts, but she pulled them altogether and absolutely wiped the floor with them and got them to pay all the costs. It was a complete rout which only she could have achieved."

"Of course," he responded. "I agree, she is an exceptional barrister, but do not underestimate your part in the victory. Together you were a superlative team."

"Well," conceded Mavis modestly. "It was so nice to win the case for the sake of Abbie and her mother whose pain in losing a father and husband was so tragic that additional pain and suffering of having to sell their family home to clear the debts was unthinkable. It was a joy to be able to help Abbie who has become a good friend to me since we began attending law classes together."

Mr Ferguson rose to leave the room.

"Yes," he said as he moved to the door. "There is always great gratification in helping one's fellows. Well done!"

Mavis continued with her work for about another half an hour until her telephone rang. She picked up the receiver and was told that there were some visitors in reception who wanted to talk to her. She strolled out into the reception area and found Charlie and Des waiting. She invited them to join her in her room which they did. Des explained what they wanted.

"I see," said Mavis rising from her chair. "I think I will have to involve Mr Ferguson, the senior partner, in this matter. I shan't be a minute."

She left them in her room while she went to find Mr Ferguson and no doubt to retrieve the conveyancing file for Mr Jones. After about five minutes she returned accompanied by her boss who was carrying a file. The introductions were made by Mavis, and everyone sat down. Des went quickly through the account of what had occurred and what it was the police needed to know. Mr Ferguson listened carefully to what Des had to say and decided that he had no objections to the contents of the file being revealed to the police. Having announced this, he left the file with Mavis and went away to his own room. Mavis opened the file and reviewed the contents and then read out to them both all the details of the Jones conveyancing file.

The papers showed that Mr Jones had instructed the firm to sell his property about three months ago and that the sale had been completed two months ago. The net value of the sale after the deduction of costs, (there had been no mortgage on the property), was £375,000.00. That sum was transferred to the bank account of Mr Jones on the completion date. The bank account was one with the HSBC bank, at the local branch. Des took a note of the account number and wondered at his powers of being able to trace the proceeds of sale beyond the local branch. He took up his mobile telephone and dialled the number of his station and spoke to his sergeant and gave him the account number of Jones' bank and asked him to set in motion enquiries to trace where the funds of his house sale had been transferred to.

Chapter 43

Des and Charlie did not go back to their respective offices but decided instead to repair to the Jubilee Inn where they could mull over the facts which they had discovered.

When they arrived Reg, the landlord was just opening up the premises. He was slightly surprised to see them at such an early hour. He cheerily greeted them both and had pulled a beer for each of them before they had discarded their coats and settled themselves down at their favourite table. They both picked an item from the early evening menu and sat down to sip from their pint glasses.

"So," said Des. "What have we got, that we didn't know before? Jones denied that he had any close knowledge of the cleaner Stephen Pike and yet we found a photo of them together posing with a fish. We have just discovered that he sold his house a couple of months ago and pocketed £375,000.00 and disappeared from the property he was renting owing one month's rent and going we know not where. How am I doing so far?"

"Spot on, I'd say," remarked Charlie. "I think it's fair to say that he was almost certainly up to no good, but there is precious little evidence to prove that the hunch is correct. In fact, were it not for his disappearance even we would be unsure of his guilt let alone a jury of twelve reasonable people."

"Absolutely," affirmed Des. "There is either something obvious that we have missed or there is something out there to be discovered which Jones knew would soon be discovered."

"Yeah," murmured Charlie nodding carefully. "But he had presumably always had the plan to make off as soon as the cash had been plundered. The question might be that his timing was always correct or as you suggest, something occurred to make him decide to leave sooner than intended."

"Hmm," said Des. "I would guess that the thing that happened, which was unforeseeable, was the heart attack of which Stephen Pike suffered while he was at the vaccination centre. Presumably, up to that point everything was going to plan; probably, after he had received his Covid jab they were supposed to meet up somewhere and then, the simple-minded Stephen would hand over to Jones the contents of his backpack."

"Yeah," said Charlie. "I reckon that you are correct. I am sure that was how it happened, but what I am unsure about is why, once it all went wrong, he decided to make his escape anyway? So far, we have not found any solid evidence to link the theft of the money to him. Presumably, if he had held his ground, he could have retained his job and the income."

"Hmm, yeah," said Des with some cynicism. "I think the truth of it was, he simply lost his nerve and since the escape route was already set up, he just felt obliged to take advantage of it. Even as we speak my sergeant is leading the investigation with the banking system to see if we can discover where he and his money have gone."

"Well," said Charlie with finality. "If I were a betting man, my money would be on him to scurry back to Hong Kong. Shall we have another drink before we go home?"

Des agreed and got to his feet to order two more beers.

Chapter 44

Mavis had been quite shocked by the visit to her office by Des and Charlie. She had not acted for Jones in his conveyancing matter. That matter had been dealt with by someone else. Although no blame had been apportioned by Des or Charlie or even hinted at, she felt some guilt about her firm's involvement with the actions of an obvious crook.

After the departure of Des and Charlie she telephoned Abbie to tell her what had happened. The latter was surprised to hear the news but not surprised to hear of any jiggery-pokery involving Mr Jones.

"I always had my suspicions about him right from the start. He was a very slimy character, and I could not bring myself to believe a single word he said."

"Well apparently, he has done a runner according to Charlie. Sold his house, (via our firm seemingly), and moved away to who knows where? We will need to meet up to have a long chat about this."

"Abbie said that she would be more than happy to meet up with her and asked when she would like to meet.

"Perhaps you would like to come round to our house this evening for a bite to eat and a drink or two?"

Abbie said she would love to do that and agreed to call at seven p.m. Consequently, at precisely that time she found herself pulling onto the driveway of George and Mavis. As she got out of her car and locked the door, she could see that the conservatory on the side of the property was all lit up and she wondered if they would be eating and drinking therein.

She rang the doorbell, and the door was answered by Mavis herself who embraced and kissed her and invited her in. She followed her into the house and through into the conservatory where a large table was already laid. There were four chairs, made of bamboo, arranged around it each with matching cushions on the seats and backs. Abbie was impressed at how attractive the area was. Mavis advised her to be careful because the floor had been washed and cleaned earlier today.

"You are amazing," Abbie assured her. "I would not have had the time at the end of a working day, to wash and clean a tiled floor of this size."

"Oh, I didn't," said Mavis. "It was George who cleaned the floor this afternoon in between giving a bedroom ceiling coats of paint."

"Wow," said Abbie with a smile. "Your millionaire husband also paints and cleans the house, while you are at work?"

"Not only that," she replied. "But he also cooks the meal for us .I am lucky I know."

She took Abbie's coat to hang it up and asked her what she would like to drink.

"Anything non-alcoholic," said Abbie. "I'm driving so would prefer not to drink."

When she returned she brought a bottle of cold tonic water and a bottle of lemonade and some chopped lemons and limes on a plate.

"I'll just get some glasses," she said. "And find out how long the food will be."

She returned with three large glasses and some ice cubes in a jar. George followed with two plates of Spaghetti Bolognese which he placed on the table and disappeared back into the kitchen and soon re-emerged with a third plate of Spaghetti and a bottle of Italian beer fresh from the fridge which he placed next to his own plate.

As they started to eat, Mavis detailed to Abbie the whole of the episode of the visit to her offices by Des and Charlie.

"Well," said Abbie. "As I told you on the phone, I always suspected he was a suspicious character. I am now confused about where I stand and what the outcome of police enquiries may reveal. I was first instructed by Mr Jones himself on behalf of the company but now it seems, the man who instructed me has disappeared. Presumably I must now report to the firm itself and no longer Mr Jones even if I knew where he was. I am still awaiting a comprehensive report by Charlie who appears to be working hand in glove with Des."

"Well," said Mavis. "I can assure you that you will never find a more reliable and conscientious investigator than Charlie. I have known him for years and know that when he reports to you it will be fully comprehensive."

"Yes," said Abbie. "I am sure you are right. He has always seemed to me to be very competent and I'm sure he will not overlook any points. I do not doubt his ability to unearth all the facts, I just worry about the circumstances when they are finally revealed. I suppose I am concerned about who I am supposed to report to now. If I send a copy of Charlie's report to whoever is in charge of the firm now that Mr Jones has disappeared, and he does not like the contents, could he refuse to pay our costs on the grounds that he had never authorised them?"

"Oh, that's a bit negative," suggested Mavis. "I'm sure that won't happen. In any event, when he gave you his instructions, he had full authority did he not?"

"Hmm," conceded Abbie grudgingly. "I suppose that's right. But I still share Charlie's misgivings, I 'm sure that there is something here that none of us knows or understands, and until we discover what that thing is there will never be a satisfactory conclusion reached. By the way George, this meal is delicious, thank you so much."

George thanked her for the compliment and said, "But why would anyone be so sure that there is anything else to discover? Surely Jones had a plan whereby he could hoodwink the cleaner (a man of limited intelligence), to steal the money for him. Part of that plan included his own escape route out of the country to a place where he could enjoy his ill-gotten gains. The plan had failed to come to fruition due to the unexpected heart attack which the cleaner suffered. That was bad luck for everyone concerned particularly Stephen Pike, but why would everyone believe that Jones would not carry out his planned escape?"

"Because," said Mavis. "He had no pile of ill-gotten gains to make off with. So why bother to escape when he could just stay in his job and continue receiving his salary?"

"Except," countered George. "If he just stayed where he was bluffing things out, and the police investigations established that he was the one to blame, he would have no place to hide would he?"

"Yes," said Abbie. "Perhaps that is all there is to it."

"Except," said Mavis. "Charlie has a feeling in his water, a suspicion which he can't put his finger on. I have worked with Charlie long enough and know him to be an extremely shrewd investigator. I have never known him to be wrong or to have an instinct which was incorrect, but Jones was intending to make off with the money he had stolen from the security firm as well as the proceeds of sale of his own house which presumably he owned lock stock and barrel."

"Or did he?" asked George with a mischievous grin.

"Of course, he did," responded Mavis. "He had a registered title in his own name. I know that because my firm acted for him when he sold it."

"But how did he pay for it when he bought it?" asked George with another mischievous grin.

"Presumably with the ill-gotten gains from his theft from the HSBC bank in Hong Kong," said Abbie, then, almost carelessly, she mused. "Always presuming that he would have been able to bring such an illegal sum of money into the UK ten years ago and if he wasn't, how could he have financed the purchase of that house?"

"Well," said George, with yet another mischievous grin. "One thing I learned when we worked in the office together, was that occasionally people were able to fraudulently transfer registered property into their names."

"Oh, surely not," said Mavis. "That is too far-fetched to be likely."

"Not really," responded George. "I read an article in the newspaper not long ago saying that such transactions were on the increase. Also, I saw a drama on TV the other day in which someone had stolen a title from someone else."

"But if it was an easy thing to do then everyone would be at it wouldn't they?" offered Mavis.

"Perhaps we ought to do some investigating into the title," said Abbie. "Except I believe it can be a difficult job delving into registered titles. The trouble is I don't know anyone who could help me."

"Oh, but I do," said Mavis.

Chapter 45

Des was in his office trying to tidy up some of his work that had suffered recently due to the fact that he had devoted most of his time to the security firm robbery case. Since his day out with Charlie the day before he was trying to catch up with his other files.

He wondered if Mr Jones had skipped the country or whether he had simply moved to another area. He was confident that his sergeant would eventually produce an answer when he had completed all the enquiries which were long and tedious. Almost on cue, there was a knock on his door and his sergeant strolled into his room carrying a file of papers.

"Well," he said scratching his own head. "We carefully checked all the aeroplane flights out of UK recently and you are not going to believe this. A few days ago, Jones took a single flight to Krakow in Poland. Don't ask me what he is doing there or whether he was merely changing flights and moving on somewhere else, e.g. Hong Kong?"

"Poland?" exclaimed Des with furrowed brow. "What is he up to?"

"Exactly," responded the sergeant. "I don't think we can go any further than that. I don't believe we have any means of tracing flights out of Poland particularly when we have no information of the intended destination."

"Well," said Des with certainty. "My money would be on him returning home to Hong Kong. It's the only place where he knows anyone. Why would he arrange to move to any place where he knew no one? Any luck on the tracing of the money from the proceeds of sale of his house?"

"We are still working on that," responded the sergeant. "I will let you know when I have any news."

"Fair enough," said Des who had already convinced himself that Jones would eventually be found back in Hong Kong. The sergeant excused himself and returned to his tracing operations. Des picked up his phone and dialled the number of his contact in the Foreign Office security service. He explained the situation and asked him to check aeroplane flights from Krakow in Poland primarily to Hong Kong, but basically to anywhere under the name of Jones. His contact promised that he would do his best but did emphasize that no promises could be made.

At the start of his day Charlie had decided to call again on the sister of Stephen Pike and in the hope that she might be at her brother's house again he drove round and parked outside the Methodist Hall. He walked up the path to the front door and pressed the bell. Stephen Pike's sister answered the door dressed in an apron and looking slightly harassed. She could not resist a sigh and a slump of the shoulders when she saw him, but managed a smile and invited him in.

They walked into the lounge which smelled of freshly applied furniture polish. She admitted to Charlie that she had been doing a lot of cleaning work with a view to selling the property. Charlie was sympathetic and explained that he was certain that her brother had not been involved in the robbery but so far, he had not quite managed to discover all the facts that would prove this. He hoped she might be able to help him prove her brother's innocence. She agreed to help him as much as possible. He asked her what evidence or records her brother had kept concerning his social life if any.

She went into the bedroom and returned carrying a cardboard box which contained papers and magazines and pens and papers.

"This is all there is," she said. "To be honest he never kept much but after he died, I collected it all and put it in this box for what it is worth. It was from here that I got that other photo I lent to the other day."

"Thanks a lot," said Charlie glancing summarily into the box. "And did he have a computer or a smart phone on which he might have kept any social history?"

"Yes," she said. "Despite his educational problems, he was quite good at working the computer. Did you want to look at that?"

"Yes, please," he said searching through the box superficially. "There doesn't appear to be anything in here so I guess, if there is anything, it will probably be on the computer."

"OK," she said. "Let's have a look at it. It is in his bedroom. I hope I can remember his password. Follow me."

They walked into what had been Stephen Pike's bedroom and his sister plugged in the computer and switched it on. They both settled down to see the contents of the e mail correspondence on the machine. She soon logged in and began to scroll through the e mails at or around the date of Stephen's death. There were a few spam calls and one or two from people who were nothing to do with Mr Jones or anyone else at the security firm. One letter writer which interested Charlie was from someone with the e mail address of *JimmyJ@hotmail.com*. Charlie pointed it out to the sister and requested her to concentrate on them.

It became apparent that 'JimmyJ' was indeed Mr Jones even though Charlie had realized that he did not know his Christian name. He was certain that it must be James. The correspondence revealed that Jones had groomed Stephen about the cash which he had told him would be left in a certain room at noon and urging him to pick it up and hide it in his backpack and that they would meet up later in the day when he would meet Stephen outside the Methodist Hall at five p.m. Charlie realized how damning the record of e mail correspondence was as far as Jones was concerned.

"I think the police will need to see this," he said. "I know it all confirms fully what the DCI believed. He will definitely want to see it." The sister said she would be quite happy to allow the police to take charge of the computer at least to prove to themselves that her brother had not been the one to blame for the theft of the money. Charlie thanked her and advised her that the police would be calling shortly to collect the computer. She suggested that he take it with him and hand it over to the police so Charlie said he would and loaded it into his car and then drove away after saying thank you to her for her assistance. Before he drove away he requested that she tell him the password of her brother in order that the police would be able to get into the machine. She gave him the information and he wrote the password into his notebook.

Chapter 46

Mavis and George were preparing for an evening out. They had both showered and changed after their working day. George had worked long and hard all day in the final bedroom of their house. He had applied another coat of white paint to the ceiling and had rubbed down the walls and skirting boards.

Mavis had worked hard in her office but found time to telephone Pete with whom she used to work. When they had worked together in their government office, Pete had been the one who continually gleaned information from the office files and had collected facts and details of many things. She knew too that he had many contacts in other government departments which enabled him to collect details of anyone and to be able to present profiles of people accordingly. He had supplied invaluable information in the past when Mavis had needed it. She told him on the phone about the man Jones who was the deputy manager of the security firm. She knew he had a contact in one of the Land Registry offices and she had hoped that he might be able to discover anything about Jones' acquisition of the property which he had recently sold. While they were talking Mavis took the opportunity to invite Pete and his new wife Sandra to meet herself and

George for a meal in the Italian restaurant La Scala that evening. Pete had readily agreed, and they arranged to meet there that evening. Pete rented a flat above the restaurant and so assured her that he would book the table and see them there at seven-thirty p.m.

When she got home from work Mavis told George about the arrangement, she had made to meet Pete and Sandra in the La Scala restaurant. He was pleased to hear this because he had not seen Pete for a few weeks. Pete was his closest friend in the office where they had all worked together. Indeed, for a while he had moved in with Pete in his flat above the Italian restaurant.

When they were both washed and freshened up George and Mavis made their way, on foot, to La Scala and took particular care to arrive on time. When they walked into the restaurant, they were greeted by the owner Fellipo who gave them an effusive welcome. He shook George's hand and hungrily kissed the hand of Mavis and declared to George, "Ah, so beautiful, you are such a lucky man."

"I know I am," said George generously, squeezing the hand of Mavis.

Fellipo led them to their table which was as always, already occupied by Pete and Sandra. They all embraced each other and George good naturedly scolded Pete for managing, yet again, to arrive before them. Pete laughed modestly and suggested that living above the restaurant gave him an unfair advantage. George and Mavis both knew that it had nothing to do with it; no matter how hard they tried, they never managed to arrive before Pete and Sandra.

They all settled down at the table and chose the drinks which they wanted and Fellipo scuttled off to fetch them. When he returned, he asked if they were ready to order their food. They each said they were and Fellipo took the order and went off to the kitchen.

"So how is everything going for you at the TV studios?" said Mavis to Sandra.

Sandra had previously been a journalist on the local paper who had been recruited by the local TV news team. Now she did news-presenting and occasional documentaries.

Sandra told her that the job with the TV company was going really well and she was loving it. She told Mavis, "I finished that documentary program about Eddie Sharp the other week I think it will be released on an obscure channel soon."

Mavis was excited to hear this. She knew all about sharp Eddie who had been a number one defendant in a couple of court cases in which Mavis herself had gathered some evidence. It was perhaps the biggest adventure of her life, and she had met her idol Phillipa Fry as a result of the activities surrounding the trials and had changed her profession thanks to an impressive reference provided by Phillipa.

George and Pete were talking between themselves about sporting things. Pete was explaining that the injury to his hand caused when he had punched one of the Gibson twins during the adventure at the Night Club just over a year or so. He asked George if he was willing to turn out for the local team for the coming rugby season. George said that he was thinking it over.

Soon Fellipo arrived with the food that they had ordered. Pete and George had ordered a pizza each. Sandra had ordered lasagne and Mavis had chosen spaghetti Bolognese. Fellipo fussed around like a mother hen sprinkling parmesan cheese on each platter.

They all tucked into their meal and gossiped so happily. Mavis reflected, while they were talking, how much she liked Pete and Sandra and realized how long it had been since they all last met. She resolved not to leave things so long until the next time they met. She said as much to them and told them how guilty she felt that what had brought them together was a favour that she had asked Pete for,

"I feel so bad," she said. "We should have been meeting up just because we love each other's company not just because I wanted some information which I knew only Pete would be able to discover."

"Talking of which," said Pete digging into his pocket and pulling out a slip of paper which he handed over to Mavis. "I had a word with my pal at the Land Registry and I think everything you need to know is written here, but you are absolutely correct, we should not leave it so long next time."

Mavis scanned the piece of paper and said, "You are so brilliant Pete, thank you so much. You were always so expert at gathering information ; I always felt that you and Charlie should have gone into business together. You are both so similar in your ability to winkle out information about anyone or anything. I know Charlie will not be surprised that this final piece of the jigsaw should be provided by you."

Inexplicably Mavis then burst into tears and covered her face with her hands. All the others were astonished and sat together dumbly wondering what to do. Sandra put her arms around her and asked her what had caused the tears.

"I'm so sorry," she said. "I was overcome with the way things have worked out. I was thinking of my friend Abbigail whose father recently took his own life. She is the one I meet at the Law lessons at the college, and she has been dealing with the matter of the missing money from the security firm which is connected to the enquiries Pete has just sorted out for me."

She drew in a breath and pulled herself together and said to George, "Well, come on my darling, time for us to go home. Ask Fellipo for the bill."

Both Pete and Sandra objected and insisted that they each pay their share but Mavis insisted that the meal was on them.

"That information you discovered for me is well worth the price of a meal," she said. "And let's face it" she said with a grin, "George can afford it."

Everyone laughed as usual especially George himself as he rustled up Fellipo and settled the bill before they all wished each other well and made their way home.

Chapter 47

When she awoke in the morning Mavis remembered that it was the day of the week when she would be going to the college and seeing Abbigail. She made a mental note to try to see Charlie first thing in the morning before she went to the college. She arrived at work extra early in her usual bid to make up for the time she lost by going to the college.

When she got to the office, she asked herself what time Charlie started work. Part of her suspected that sometimes he slept in his office perhaps because he simply couldn't be bothered to go home to his lonely flat. She thought she would try to telephone him and did so, not really expecting him to answer.

"Chivers' detective agency," came the instant reply.

Mavis was so surprised to hear him reply that she couldn't reply instantly.

"Chivers' detective agency!" Charlie repeated with extra volume.

"Oh, hello Charlie," she said. "I wasn't sure if you would be in this early."

"Hello, Mavis," he replied. "What can I do for you?"

"Well," she told him, "it's more what I can do for you. Can I pop up and speak to you for a few minutes.?"

"Yes of course," he said. "See you in a second."

Mavis climbed the stairs clutching a photocopy of the slip of paper which Pete had given her the evening before. When she reached Charlie's room she became more convinced that he sometimes slept in the office. The clothes he wore did not look like clothes freshly selected that morning from a reservoir of freshly laundered items. He also had a shadowy stubble on his chin and altogether gave the impression of someone who had just awoken and was unwashed. Despite this Charlie himself looked as mentally alert as ever.

"Good morning, Mavis, you are up and about bright and early today."

"Yeah," she replied. "Today is the day I go to the college for a lesson day. I like to come in early to make up for the time I am away from the office. Call it a guilt feeling if you like. I will be seeing Abbigail while I'm there. I will be giving her a copy of this when we meet and I wanted to be able to assure her that you had already received it."

She passed the slip of paper across his desk and Charlie read it. He nodded his head knowingly.

"I always knew there was something else about him. This is dynamite isn't it? How did you get hold of this?"

"Where else," she responded. "I got it from Pete who has a friend or colleague who works in the Land Registry."

"Wow," muttered Charlie. "No wonder he wanted or needed to leave the country post haste."

"Indeed," said Mavis. "Well, I'd better be off, I have plenty to do before I have to go to the college."

She left Charlie to peruse the information she had passed to him under the weather eye of the calendar girl. She knew that he would soon be reporting to Des and to Abbigail whom she herself would soon be meeting up with. She returned to her office on the ground floor and did some work on one or two files which were on her desk. After an hour or so she packed up her papers and placed them in her brief case and made her way to the college.

When she arrived, she seated herself at a desk and deposited her Brief case on the chair next to her by way of reserving that space for Abbie who had not so far arrived. Shortly thereafter Abbie arrived and sat beside her. Mavis handed her a copy of the information slip of paper which Pete had given to her. She explained that the details came direct from a pal of Pete who worked in the Land Registry but none of the information was official.

Abbie read through the note and raised her eyebrows and breathed out deeply.

"Wow," she said. "That is quite shocking, though I am not sure where it leaves us in respect of the general investigations in respect of the loss of the money."

"Well," replied Mavis. "I can tell you that I gave a copy of this to Charlie earlier this morning, and no doubt it will be included in his final report to you when it arrives. You know that he has a contact in the local CID who will no doubt be interested to learn about this."

Just as she said this the lecturer entered the classroom and their day's lesson began. Today's subject was criminal law. Both Abbie and Mavis both reflected that the subject matter of today's lecture was entirely appropriate to what they were experiencing in real life. The morning seemed, to both of them, to fly by and before they knew it the lunchtime break was upon them, and they repaired to their favourite coffee/ snack bar.

As they settled down to enjoy their coffee and sandwiches Abbie in between bites of her sandwich, remarked, "Well, I always knew that Jones character was suspect, but this information proves it beyond all doubt."

"Yes," agreed Mavis. "I thought you would say something like that, and it just goes to show how accurate your initial impression of the man was."

As she said this, Mavis looked at her watch and said, "I think we should be going back to the college otherwise we will be late for our afternoon session."

They both got to their feet and headed back towards the college, chatting away as they went.

Chapter 48

Charlie was not at his best this morning. He had woken up to find that his throat was sore. He did not feel gravely ill but did not, at the same time, feel one hundred percent well. Normally, he would start the working day with a cup of strong tea and one of his Manakin cigars but today the ache in his throat forbade him from lighting up a cigar.

He checked the information provided by Pete the details of which had been provided by someone working inside the Land Registry. He knew that he would have to discuss this with Des as soon as possible. He looked at his watch and decided that it was too early in the morning to ring Des. He looked through the paperwork on his desk and settled down to working meticulously through each of the documents.

After all, he thought to himself, *One still had to make a living.* He glanced up at the picture of the calendar girl on his wall and reflected on how, in many ways, life had passed him by. He knew that he was too old to hope that he could ever share his life with an angel like her. He realized, as he looked at her picture, that his own estranged daughter would by now be about the same age. Where had the time gone, he thought.

Des was in his office and working hard on a statement which he hoped would be signed by an unfortunate who was currently cooling his heels in a cell having been arrested late last night. Des knew that the man was guilty as charged but had preferred to let him rest in the cell for a few hours before speaking to him. He regarded this as a softening up process and was so confident of the procedure that he was currently preparing the man's statement before even conducting a formal interview with him. Such was the confidence of Des in his own ability and experience. It was not unusual for him to proceed in this fashion and very seldom was he ever disappointed with his own efforts. As he was finishing the statement he paused for a breath and his telephone rang. He picked up the receiver and spoke into it, "O'Nighons speaking," he said confidentially.

"Hi Des it's me," said Charlie. "Are you busy?" he interrupted the call to cough persistently.

"Oh dear," commented Des as he listened to Charlie painfully hacking. "Yeah I'm free now, just finishing a job. Shall we meet at the Jubilee in ten minutes time?"

"OK," said Charlie and put down the phone. He gathered up his paperwork and popped them into his battered old briefcase along with his Daily Mail and the extra copy of the information given by Pete. He reached for his raincoat and gave the calendar girl a gesture by touching his brow with his forefinger in a farewell salute. He then left his office and made his way to the Jubilee Inn. As usual, it took him about ten to twelve minutes walking to reach the doors of the Jubilee Inn. He walked into the bar and was greeted as usual by Reg Partridge the smiling rosy faced landlord.

"How are you today Charlie?" he asked as he automatically reached for a glass and began pouring a glass of his favourite beer.

"Oh, I'm all right thanks, Reg," he replied unconvincingly. "I think I've managed to pick up a cold or mild dose of the flu but otherwise I'm OK."

"Well," said Reg looking concerned. "It could be Covid of course, have you taken a test to make sure?"

"No," replied Charlie without any great conviction. "I recognise the symptoms and they are the same as every cold or flu I suffer every winter."

Reg looked unconvinced and said. "Well," he said. "You do know don't you that the Covid bug can imitate a cold or flu exactly. Do you have any of the testing kits?"

Charlie looked decidedly disinterested and said, "Nah, I'll be all right in a few days."

"No," insisted Reg authoritatively. "It's not wise to take any risks. After all, if you are carrying the bug, even if you feel OK, you could be passing it on to others. I don't want all my clientele infected by you. My wife has a box of test kits out the back. I'll get her to bring one out in a minute and we'll test you. Just to be safe."

Charlie reluctantly said OK and took his beer to the table and opened his Daily Mail and began reading. After about five minutes Des walked in and bought himself a pint at the bar and then joined Charlie at the table.

"How are you doing?" he asked Charlie. "I see that Reg has got cottage pie on the lunchtime menu. Did you fancy some?"

Charlie said he did so Des wandered over to the bar and ordered two cottage pies with chips and peas and paid Reg the money. He returned to the table and sat down.

"So," he said to Charlie. "What was it you wanted to tell me?"

Charlie slid across the table the copy of the information which Pete had obtained from the Land Registry. Des read it all carefully with raised eyebrows. Then he read it all again and gave a low whistle.

"Well, that answers a few of the questions that we have had for quite a while."

Charlie nodded. "Yeah, it seems that Jones previously rented a property from an elderly guy who was a widower and somehow managed to winkle his way in with the chap and persuaded him into transferring the property into his name for a peppercorn and somehow got it past the HM Land Registry without any inquiries and as soon as the property was transferred into his name he promptly sold it again straight away and then left the country."

"Yeah," confirmed Des. "And only after he had fled the country did some distant relatives of the old guy come out of the woodwork and accuse the Land Registry of negligence etc. How and where did you manage to get all this information?"

Charlie explained that the information had come from Pete, "You remember, he was the chap that gathered all that information in the Eddie Sharp case before it went to trial. He used to work with Mavis in the government office remember?"

"Yes, of course," said Des. "A very thorough and resourceful individual but I recall that most of the information which he obtained was achieved by nefarious means. I presume that these details were also obtained by the same means."

Charlie nodded. "Yeah, that's right, couldn't be used in a court of law. But what about in the Eddie Sharp trials? Didn't you get your officer(s), to render statements to say this was the information they personally had collected?"

"True," said Des without shame. "But I am always nervous about presenting a case with that sort of evidence. Anyway, it may already be too little too late. My sergeant has discovered that the money from Jones' bank account was transferred to the Commonwealth bank in Australia. The bad news is that he has obviously done a final bunk, but the good news (if there is any), is that it looks as though he has decided to settle in a commonwealth country. For what it's worth, it may be slightly easier to track him down in Australia than inside the Chinese empire."

Their conversation was interrupted by the arrival of Reg's wife from the kitchen with their cottage pies. She presented the plates to them then produced from her apron pocket the Covid testing device which she opened for Charlie to use. He gave a disappointed groan and pushed aside the packet and preferred to wield his knife and fork but Reg's wife was having none of it. She picked up the swab device and demanded that Charlie opened his mouth wide. He did as he was told and she took the sample and then applied it to the testing device. She frowned noticeably and declared that it was positive. She went over to her husband at the bar counter to show him the evidence. Reg himself came over to their table and announced confidentially to Charlie, "I'm afraid it is positive, Charlie. I suggest that you finish your meal and then go straight home and isolate for about five days."

Charlie shrugged his shoulders frustratedly and continued with his cottage pie and looked toward Des and said, "Well, how bloody annoying is that? I don't need all this. I've got work to do. I can't lock myself up for a week."

Des looked sympathetic but felt, as a police officer, he could not advise Charlie to do other than Reg had told him. As he watched Charlie wolfing down his cottage pie, he reflected that one of the symptoms of Covid was certainly not loss of appetite. He concluded to Charlie, "I have decided to diplomatically exclude from my final report that Phil the taxi driver was in any way connected to the disappearance of the money. I will merely observe that the backpack was found, and record the amount that was found in it. The firm will have to be content to have recovered the majority of the money and will no doubt be compensated by their insurance company for the relatively small amount which had been spent. It might be a good idea if, while you are isolating, you prepare your final report and present a similar final report."

Chapter 49

Abbie had experienced a gruelling day at the office. She had several complicated reports that she had to draw up and had made, she complimented herself, a good job of all of them. She hoped that Mr Morris would agree. In fairness he had yet to criticise any work which she had so far turned out but she knew that she was always one step away from a glaring error.

When she arrived home from the office, she found her mother in a buoyant mood. She had just returned from a session of aerobic exercises at the gym and began telling Abbie all about the other ladies in her class, and the instructor, a middle-aged lady who Stephanie thought was inspiring.

Abbie was so pleased to note the optimistic mood of her mother. She reflected that it was only a short time ago, after the death of her father, and following the shocking information of his gambling debts, that her mother's mood had been at such a low ebb. Now, she seemed to have almost recovered completely from the whole affair.

Her mother quickly rustled up a pasta salad and sprinkled some parmesan cheese onto it and they both sat at the kitchen table happily munching away and chatting contentedly. Abbie told her that her friend Joyce had arranged to call round in the evening. They both finished their salad and then Stephanie found a couple of packets of yoghurt with fruit sauce from the depths of her fridge.

Shortly after, the doorbell rang, and Abbie went to answer it. Joyce was waiting on the doorstep, and they were happy to see each other. After an embrace, Abbie led her through to the kitchen area where Stephanie was doing the washing up. They both said hello and Joyce seated herself on a kitchen stool. Abbie searched the wine rack and produced a bottle of Rose wine from Italy. She opened the bottle and poured a glass for each of them. They chatted away for about twenty minutes and then Abbie announced that they would be going up to her bedroom for a girlie chat. They topped up their glasses and then went upstairs to Abbie's bedroom. As they sat down Joyce asked Abbie, "Have you had any more conversations with that plumber? The one with the boat?"

"No," said Abbie. "To be honest I've been a bit preoccupied with family things and work. I was going to go on the laptop and see if there was anything from him." She picked up the laptop and switched it on and began the log-in process. Joyce seemed beside herself with information which she gave her now, "I've just found myself a new boyfriend." She looked so pleased with herself.

"Really?" said Abbie with surprise in her voice. "Wow, that's a big surprise, when did that happen?"

"Just the other day," she replied. "I was at my gym, and he hit upon me. He is an instructor at the gym, he is really fit and ripped. I couldn't believe it."

"What's he like?" Abbie asked. "What's his name?"

"Carlos?" she replied. "He's from Spain. He's been in this country for about five years, three of which he spent in college learning English language. At the end of his college period, he decided to stay in UK and found himself a job at the gym where he hit upon me. I'm so excited."

"And how old is this, Romeo?" asked Abbie with a feeling of apprehension.

"He's twenty-two," said Joyce.

"So, six years younger than you?" noted Abbie.

"Oh, don't be judgemental" said Joyce. "We get on so well together, age doesn't matter that much."

"That's OK then," said Abbie without too much enthusiasm. "Just follow your heart and have a good time."

"Thanks," said Joyce. "But let's see what we can do to liven up your love life, shall we?"

Abbie smiled and concentrated as the computer joined her up with the site of Pete the plumber. There was a message waiting for her saying that he (Pete), would be pleased to meet her any weekend she chose and giving her directions as to how to find his boat. He also assured her that if the weather was really bad then he would enjoy entertaining her on board.

"I bet he would," said Joyce with a cynical air, then as if sensing that her remark might have been unnecessary. "

I mean, the boat is probably quite comfortable, like a small bed-sit?"

Abbie didn't look totally convinced but said, "I suppose you could be right. Shall I give it a chance and see how it goes? After all, if the boat or him looks dreadful I can always jump back into my car and scuttle off back home, can't I?"

Joyce's face lit up, she said, "That's the spirit. Nil desperandum! Go for it, but try not to give him those vibes about maybe running straight back to your car. Try to be positive and enthusiastic."

Eventually, after one or two stumbling starts, with some judicious editing from Joyce, Abbie managed to send a bright and breezy reply to Pete, telling him how much she was looking forward to seeing him and his boat and awaiting details as to how to find it.

Chapter 50

Charlie was in his office. He had been there all night and was not feeling too well. He had typed up his report on his old-fashioned typewriter and was reviewing it now. He had made sure that his version of events coincided with those of Des which he already knew. While he was reviewing the report, he reflected on how unwell he was feeling. For the last two days he had experienced a sore throat and now he felt as if every muscle and joint in his body ached. He also had an intense headache and a fever. The last time he had felt like this was when he had contracted a strong dose of influenza.

So, he thought to himself, *Is this a dose of Covid which I have, or is it just a good old-fashioned flu?*

Charlie placed his report into a large envelope along with his invoice addressed to the firm of Featherstones. He reached into his drawer and found a book of stamps and licked one and stuck it onto the envelope. He dragged himself to his feet and went out of his office and walked down to the street level. He wandered out onto the pavement and walked the few yards to the post box and pushed the envelope into it. He turned, breathed in deeply and then walked back to the office and climbed the staircase to the top of the building and entered his office.

He was breathing heavily and slumped onto the settee which was against one wall of the room and under the window. He looked across at the wall opposite him and noticed the calendar girl still smiling at him. He smiled gently and closed his eyes and immediately feel asleep.

A day or two later Abbie received the envelope at her office and was intrigued and disappointed by the fact that Charlie had sent it to her in the post. She had expected that when she received his report, it would be hand delivered by Charlie himself. She tried to speak to him on the phone but could not get a reply from him. Eventually she telephoned Mavis and explained matters to her and asked if she had seen Charlie in the last few days. Mavis said she had not seen him for a few days but would immediately pop upstairs and look for him.

She put down the phone and immediately made her way up the stairs towards Charlie's office on the third floor of the building. When she reached the door to his office she paused and listened to see if she could hear any noise from inside. All was silent and she knocked gently on the door and waited for a response. She heard nothing and so she tentatively tried the door handle and gave a gentle push. The door opened silently, and Mavis crept into the office area calling out Charlie's name.

The light in the office was dingy and the room smelled stale. Charlie's desk was jumbled up with paperwork and general office stationery detritus including half-empty coffee cups and a half-bottle of scotch whiskey. The room appeared at first to be empty and she moved to the window and pulled at the blind to admit daylight into the office. As she did so she discerned a groan or sigh emanate from a bundle of rags or clothes on the sofa beneath the window.

When she looked more closely, and as the daylight permitted a better view, she realized that the bundle of rags was indeed Charlie dressed in his usual office attire. His eyes were closed but she was unable to tell if he was unconscious generally, or merely simply asleep. She gave his shoulder a gentle shake and murmured his name, but the recumbent figure did not stir. She shook him a bit harder and called his name louder but still no re-action from him. She touched his forehead and noticed that he felt very hot and was obviously suffering with a fever.

She went over to his desk and telephoned for an ambulance. She went into his modest toilet with hand basin in it and found a flannel in the basin which she soaked with cold water. She returned to the unconscious Charlie and applied the flannel to his forehead. She pressed the flannel into his mouth and squeezed some cold water into his throat which he appeared to drink. She assessed the situation and decided to return to her office temporarily in order to tell everyone what had happened and to ask them all to keep a look out for the ambulance when it arrived. One of the staff had some experience of first aid and accompanied her back up the stairs to take a look at Charlie. This lady tried to awaken him and concluded that he was unconscious, and that Mavis had done the right thing in calling for an ambulance. They both waited with the patient until the ambulance arrived and watched as the two ambulancemen carried Charlie downstairs on a stretcher.

After the ambulance drove off Mavis returned to her office and telephoned Abbigail to advise her what had happened, "I am not sure what exactly was wrong with him, all I know is he was unconscious. One of our ladies here who has had first aid training, had a look at him. Anyway, he's gone to the hospital, so we'll find out later what is wrong with him. I think I will give Des a ring at the local police station and let him know. He might have some idea what might be wrong with him. They usually see each other quite often. Probably, he was the last person to have seen him conscious."

After finishing her call with Abbie she telephoned the police station and spoke to Des who fortunately was in his office. She told him what had happened with Charlie and the fact that he was now in the local hospital.

"I'm not sure what is wrong with him, but he was unconscious and suffering with a fever."

"It's Covid," Des told her and then explained about what had happened two days before in the Jubilee Inn. "When I said farewell to him, he was creeping off to rest in bed and isolate for a few days. You had better get yourself tested if you have just spent an hour or so close to him."

Mavis agreed with him and said she would test herself as soon as possible and that she would telephone the hospital and let them know about Charlie probably suffering from Covid. Des said that after seeing Charlie, he had tested himself but had produced a negative result. Mavis rounded off the conversation by promising to phone him again as soon as she had any further information about Charlie's condition.

Having said goodbye to Des, Mavis telephoned the hospital to inform them that the patient who had just been admitted by ambulance was almost certainly suffering from Covid.

Chapter 51

That evening Abbie went online in her bedroom and contacted Pete the plumber on her laptop. This was the first time she had ever been onto the site without the assistance of Joyce, and she was feeling quite adventurous to be doing it by herself.

She noted that there was a reply from Pete telling her that he was delighted to have heard from her in the positive way that she had replied and giving her a list of dates which would be acceptable to him for a meet-up. He explained that any gaps in the calendar were due to weekends that he had already pencilled in to meet his children. He invited her to choose one of the dates and said he was hoping to meet her. She was quite touched by the thoughtful nature of his messages and concluded that he seemed to be a nice all-round sort of guy.

She took the bull by the horns and chose the first - available weekend on the list he had provided, and asked if there was anything that he would like her to bring with her e.g. food etc. He soon replied, saying that there was already plenty of fresh food on the boat due to the fact that his children would usually stay with him on the boat on alternative weekends. He gave her the exact address of where the boat was moored together with the post-code, and asked what time she was likely to arrive.

Abbie sent him a reply saying she would be there at about ten a.m. and then began to gnaw at her knuckles in case she had made a terrible mistake. She knew that she would not know this unless and until she made the journey to the boat. She made a promise to herself that even though she was fairly certain that Pete was a nice guy, she would give Joyce all the details as to where the boat was situated and further, that she would phone her when she got to the boat to confirm that all was OK. If she (Joyce), did not receive a phone call from her, then she could initiate a search party. She thought, while she was thus reflecting, that this plan was slightly negative in nature but nevertheless felt it was better to be safe than sorry.

The following morning it was the day on which she went to the college and when she arose she looked forward to meeting up with Mavis when she got there. In accordance with her usual practise she arrived extra early at her office in order to do some useful work before leaving to go to the college. As always, she was the first to arrive and settled down to some work but was somewhat surprised to hear someone else in the building. There was a soft knock on her door and then in walked Mr Morris who yet again emphasized that it was not necessary for her to come to work so early just because it was her college day. Abbie started to justify her position but he held up his hand and assured her that she was not obliged to come in early but her conscientious attitude was noted.

She passed a copy of Charlie's report across the desk and said, "This is a copy of the report by Charlie in respect of the security firm theft which I was just reading."

Mr Morris took about ten minutes to read it and nodded.

"Hmm," he said, quite interesting. "I presume the police will have considerable difficulty in tracking down Mr Jones, if ever. I suppose it is relatively good news that most of the money was recovered."

Abbie nodded, and then told him about the circumstances of Charlie who had been rushed into hospital the day before.

"I am sorry to hear that," he said. "He is a nice man and I hope he recovers soon. This epidemic is really very serious, isn't it?"

Again, Abbie nodded and said, "As you say, there appears to be little or no chance of Mr Jones being apprehended, so I presume that our business with the firm must now be at an end? Should I prepare a final invoice and send it to the manager of the company?" Mr Morris also nodded and instructed her to do so. Shortly after he went to his own office to commence his day's work. Abbie got herself ready to go to the college.

When she arrived she found Mavis was already there. She seated herself alongside her and as she greeted her she unloaded her paperwork onto the desk. The first thing she mentioned to Mavis was the occurrence of the day before.

"So, what news do you have of Charlie?" she asked. "Did the hospital have anything to say yesterday?"

"No," said Mavis with a shake of her head. "He remained unconscious until the close of the day. They did do a further test on him and confirmed that he still had Covid. I will call at the hospital later today to find out if there is any improvement."

Just then the lecturer entered the classroom, and the lesson began, and the girls had no more time for a chat.

Chapter 52

After her day at college, Mavis made a detour on her way home and visited the hospital to find out how Charlie was getting on. She parked in the hospital car park and made her way to the entrance door where she found out that things were not quite so straight forward as the last time, she had visited Charlie in hospital. That time had been when he had got injured following a disagreement with one of the twins at the flat belonging to a young lady with whom one of the twins had fathered a child. The twin had been battering on her door when Mavis and Charlie had arrived and during a struggle the twin had swept Charlie aside and he had fallen and broken two ribs. When Mavis visited him then she was able to stroll into the hospital unchallenged and find her own way towards the ward and bed in which Charlie had been located.

This time however, due to the added concern by the hospital authority she was met by a desk barring the entrance and was subjected to an interrogation as to who she was visiting and why. She gave all the information regarding Charlie but had to concede that she was not related to Charlie. She could see the direction the conversation was taking, so decided to expand on the truth a bit. She told them that they worked together, and that

Charlie had no living relatives and was no doubt in need of some comfort from a friendly face and that she was the closest person in the world for him. She was also asked about whether she had been tested for Covid and was able to produce on her phone the evidence that she had been injected twice. That seemed to satisfy her interrogator who allowed her to proceed to the Covid ward and was given a mask to wear and then permitted to approach his bed but not to touch him.

Mavis viewed the demeanour of her friend and if she was honest with herself, she did not like what she saw. His countenance was pasty, and his face was lined in places where she had not seen lines before. He looked ten years older than when she had last seen him. His breathing was laboured and with each breath he made a rasping sound. Clearly, he was unconscious, but Mavis had no way of knowing if he had remained unconscious from the moment he arrived at hospital or whether he had awoken earlier and gone back to sleep. She searched the ward and found a nurse and asked her about Charlie's circumstances. The nurse explained that Charlie had not so far regained consciousness and certainly, was not expected to. He was connected up to breathing tubes and had liquid dripping into his arm from a reservoir of solution suspended above him.

Mavis looked at him sorrowfully and decided that she would not stay any longer but would go home. She would check his progress the following day. When she did get home, she telephoned Des to tell him that she had just been into the hospital, but Charlie had not re-gained consciousness.

"I'm a bit worried about him," she said. "I remember how sick he looked when he was in hospital after the twin had injured him, but he looks even worse to me this time. If you care about him Des, you'll please keep an eye out for him. I don't think he has anyone else who cares about him."

"Yeah, OK," agreed Des. "Thanks a lot for your involvement and concern."

After he put the phone down Des reflected on what Mavis had said. He knew before she had mentioned it, that Charlie had no close friend in his life except for Des himself. They had been fellow officers in the CID many years before, and even though Charlie had left the service, they had remained friends and because of the affinity of their respective jobs they continued to meet, almost daily, usually in the Jubilee Inn. As he reflected on this fact, he realized how important the relationship was for him and presumably Charlie as well.

Chapter 53

The following Saturday morning at nine o'clock in the morning, Abbie set off in the direction of Bristol having entered into her satellite navigation device the information Pete the plumber has sent her a few days before. Although, in one sense she was looking forward to this adventure, on the other hand she was, understandably, rather nervous. On the evening before she had telephoned Joyce to make sure she knew what was going on. Joyce re-assured her that she was fully in the know and would be expecting to receive from her two telephone calls from her on Saturday morning, one at ten a.m. approximately confirming that she had arrived at the boat belonging to Pete the plumber. The second telephone call she would be expecting would be about half an hour later confirming that she had met up with Pete and that he seemed to be trustworthy. If she did not receive either or both of those calls, she confirmed that she would alert the emergency services.

Although Abbie was reasonably re-assured by this arrangement, she still admitted to herself that she was nervous. She had never previously been on a blind date and so was nervous about the whole procedure. She had no idea of how well the meeting would go. She supposed that unless Pete was a naturally predatory person, that he too would probably be equally nervous.

On the other hand, she tried to cheer herself up by noting that the weather that morning was bright and sunny, and no doubt would be the perfect day for a trip on a boat. She switched on her radio and located a music channel and began to forget about her nerves and just hum along to the music coming out of the radio.

It took her just under an hour to make the journey. Her sat-nav device took her alongside the river Avon near Bristol and she parked close to an area where there were several boats moored. She got out of her car and wandered along the pavement looking at each boat in turn. There were a few boats all moored close to each other, but on only one boat was anyone on board. He was a man of about thirty-five to forty years of age. He wore a T shirt and blue jeans and had a suntanned face, which due to the time of year was unusual. Abbie thought that his weatherworn face reflected the many trips to sea which he obviously made. Either that, or he had just returned from a foreign holiday. He was preoccupied, coiling up a length of rope and did not at first see her standing there. She stood there silent and nervous and could not work up the courage to speak or decide to move on before he saw her.

Eventually, perhaps, he sensed her there and looked up. Immediately he flashed a bright smile revealing perfectly white even teeth.

"Abbie?" he enquired getting to his feet as she nodded imperceptibly. "Nice to see you. Please come on board, let me show you around."

He moved towards a very temporary and insecure-looking gang-plank which was nothing more than a piece of plywood which had been cut off of a bigger sheet and was merely leaning across from the shore to the edge of the boat. Pete reached out a hand and helped her across the plank. She was aware, as he held her hand and she held his arm with her free hand, that he was strong. His arm felt like whip chord although Pete himself did not look overtly muscular. She landed safely on the deck of his boat and for an embarrassing moment they stood looking at each other without speaking.

Pete broke the silence by saying, "So the directions I sent you were helpful for you?"

Abbie confirmed that they were and that she had had a pleasant trouble free journey.

"Right," he said rubbing his hands together. "I'll show you around, follow me, and mind your head all the way."

Ducking down he led the way down the steps into the cabin which was small but neat. There were two bench seats, one each side which presumably could be used as a bed when his children were on board. At the end of the cabin was a table and a sink for cooking purposes, and beyond that a door which he opened and invited her to look inside. She peered into the room and was surprised to see a double bed, made up and looking inviting. She was impressed to see some cupboards squeezed into the spaces on each side of the bed and above and behind the head of the bed. She was reminded of a motor home caravan that she had looked inside once and was completely surprised at the ingenuity of the design. She said as much to Pete who nodded.

"Yeah," he agreed. "They are all beautifully designed, and it is surprising how much it is possible to squeeze in. Some people spend their whole life living in a boat not much bigger than this."

They walked back to the main cabin area and seated themselves down on the benches. Pete asked her if she would like a cup of coffee and she said that would be nice. He rose and went to the sink and filled the kettle and got some cups out of a storage cupboard. While he was making the coffee he explained to her that, due to the fact that there was no wind today, it would make sailing the boat virtually impossible. He suggested that they could have their coffee on deck in the sunshine. Abbie nodded in agreement.

"There is a very nice pub along the road which has a lovely garden restaurant which is so enjoyable on a sunny day like today. If you like we could stroll along there and have a casual lunch."

Abbie said that sounded good and so they went back up the steps to sit on the deck and drink their coffee. Sitting in the sunshine Abbie felt completely at ease. It was only when Pete took the coffee cups downstairs to wash them up that she remembered her promise to ring Joyce. She retrieved her phone from her handbag and phoned her friend who answered immediately.

"I was just about to alert the emergency services," said Joyce. "What's he like?"

"OK," said Abbie. "I've not been here that long. Nice old boat in very clean and tidy order. He seems very nice, but we are still feeling our way. There is no breeze for sailing, so we are going down the road to a pub for lunch and a chat. I'll fill you in with all the details next time I see you. Are you seeing the Spaniard today?"

"No," replied Joyce. "he's working at the gym all day today. Saturday is their busiest day of the week. I won't be seeing him at all today unless I book into one of his exercise classes but I'm not sure I want to do that today. Anyway, shall I come round on Monday evening, then you can tell me all about the rest of your day with Pete the plumber."

That was agreed and Abbie switched off her phone and replaced it in her handbag as Pete was coming back up the steps.

Chapter 54

Charlie's progress in the hospital was painfully slow. His response to treatment was virtually zero. The hospital staff were extremely concerned about his condition. They had tested every aspect of his health and had attached to him all manner of tubes and wires and devices. The chief consultant had made the decision to place him into a coma for his own good, but no one could decide how long he should be left in that condition. Nobody was expert enough to know how long he should be left unconscious, but everyone agreed that he was safer as he was. Probably, they felt, a week might do it, but if things did not improve, he could be kept alive and as healthy as possible in all the circumstances for at least six months without having to make another decision.

Mavis was very worried about him and checked with the hospital each day to check on his condition. She was also in constant contact with Des to inform him what she had discovered every morning and to find out if Des had heard anything about their mutual friend. Des was also very concerned about Charlie and, unlike Mavis, he checked in with the hospital every evening so that each time they spoke daily on the telephone, it was always likely that one of them might have some news for the other.

Des was also very concerned and extremely worried about the progress, or rather the lack of progress, in Charlie's recovery. The longer the detective lingered the more Des realized how important to him his longstanding colleague was. He attended at Charlie's hospital bed at the end of each working day and sat watching his laboured breathing and reminiscing about episodes they had experienced together.

One of the days when he was doing this a young man in a white coat with a stethoscope around his neck came to the bedside and checked the details of Charlie's chart which was hung over the foot of his bed. He stared at Charlie as if trying to decide on something. Des watched him and said, "What do you think? I assume you are his doctor. How is he doing?"

The young man gripped an ID which was hanging around his neck alongside the stethoscope and showed it to Des who examined it to find that the young man was a registrar by the name of Dolling. Des whipped out his own ID card and flashed it to Mr Dolling as he had done to so many suspects in the past. The young registrar glanced at the ID presented by Des and asked surprisingly, "Oh, are you a Mason?" And then when Des looked totally nonplussed. "It's just that I heard or read somewhere that a majority of high-ranking police officers join the Masons, I know that one of our senior consultants is a Mason and meets and knows many of your colleagues."

Des responded that he was not in the Masons nor ever considered joining them.

"However," he said. "Charlie here used to be a colleague of mine in the police force. He is now a private investigator but still helps us out often with local matters. I would personally be very grateful if you would do all you can for him."

Mr Dolling gave him a knowing look and a nod.

"I was just pondering the case," he said. "I was considering if it was time to withdraw him from his coma. I think he is virtually there and might be ready to re-gain full consciousness."

Des brightened up immediately and told the registrar, who, now he examined him more closely, did not look quite so young as he had first supposed.

"I am sure you are right," he said. "He is a real fighter you know. You can't bring him back too soon. He will relish being back in the real world and won't let you down."

Mr Dolling considered this for a moment and said, "Yes, I think you may be right. Perhaps now is the time to bring him out of his coma. I will talk to my colleague about it and maybe later today we can bring him back."

Des smiled and shook his hand and told him he was pleased that he had made that decision, and he knew also that Charlie himself would, if he were conscious, be grateful too.

"I know that you have made a good decision here," he said. "And my regards also to your consultant who is in the Masons. I believe that most of the police force who are members, joined for political reasons, but I am sure your colleague would have joined for more altruistic reasons."

Having said that he left the ward, promising himself that probably tomorrow he would be able to have a conversation with Charlie and how much he would enjoy that.

Chapter 55

Mavis woke early as always and rose before George. She showered and dressed while he was still asleep. She had two reasons to be up early, firstly it was the day of the week on which she went to college. Like her friend Abbie, she felt guilty about taking time off work even though that time was spent learning how to be a better lawyer. Nevertheless, she felt guilty and preferred to attend her office early to try to do extra work to make up for the time she was at the college in the same way as her friend Abbie did. Also, she wanted to leave her house early to pop into the hospital in order to check on Charlie, but she knew that the visit would only be brief because he was permanently unconscious.

She was just munching some cereal and drinking a glass of orange juice, when George wandered into the kitchen area wearing just a pair of underpants.

"You're up early today," he said kissing her on the cheek and opening the fridge. He gulped from the bottle of orange juice.

"Yeah," said Mavis. "It's my college day so I want to do some work at the office first and I also want to check on Charlie."

"But," he said. "Charlie's in a coma, there is no point in calling in to see him surely, just a phone call would be sufficient?"

"Yeah, I know," she said. "But I just feel so bad about not visiting him personally."

George shrugged his shoulders and reflected that his wife's truculence or her stubbornness was part of what made him love her. He put his arms around her, kissed her neck and whispered to her, "That's OK honey, I understand how you feel. Charlie is lucky to have a friend like you."

She turned to him and gave him a kiss on the lips and said, "Thanks, darling for understanding me. I am so lucky to have you and I love you so much."

She collected up her handbag and briefcase and put her arms around George again and said, "Goodbye darling, I won't be too late tonight."

She left the house and got in her car and drove first to the local hospital where she parked in the main car park and made her way to the ward where Charlie was. She donned her Covid facemask and entered the ward and made her way to Charlie's bed. She sat herself down on a chair beside his bed and looked at him. To her immense surprise, her eyes met his looking back at her. She was so shocked that initially she was unable to speak. Her mouth opened in surprise, and she mouthed, "Hello Charlie, how are you? Are you OK?"

Charlie managed a faint smile and an even fainter nod, but he offered no words. Mavis gleefully grasped his hand and gently squeezed it. She felt a gentle response and was so excited that she kissed him on the cheek and told him how happy she was to see him back. Charlie never moved or spoke but just stayed exactly where he was with his eyes fixed firmly upon her. The initial joy which Mavis had felt when she saw that the detective was conscious, was diluted by the realization that he was unable to speak. She patted his hand and told him she was going to seek out a nurse. She went to the desk inside the doorway to the ward which was manned by two nurses. She spoke to them for a few moments and learned that Charlie had been brought out of the coma the previous evening and appeared to be in a reasonable medical condition but confirmed that he appeared to have lost the power of speech. She said that tests would be carried out in due course to see exactly what his present condition and the possibility of a full recovery was.

Mavis made her way back to Charlie's bed and assured him that she would be back later in the day to see him but now she had to go somewhere. She then made her way out to the carpark and before driving to her office she dialled the number of Des who answered immediately. She told him what she had found when visiting Charlie this morning.

"The only problem Des is that he cannot or does not talk at the moment although the nurse has told me that this is not necessarily too serious because he may regain the power of speech later."

Des said he thought that was great news and that he would be visiting Charlie after work today. Mavis told him that she also might return after work so would see him there. After hanging up her phone call she made her way to her office to do an hour or so of work before attending the college for her weekly law lesson.

She was pleased as usual to meet Abbie there and they sat together as always. She told Abbie all about Charlie whom she had just seen at the hospital. Abbie was thrilled to hear the news but slightly anxious to hear that he could not speak. The lesson started promptly on time and both girls were introduced to the Tort of Nuisance. After two hours of Nuisance, they were both ready for some lunch and went to their usual coffee bar.

"So why do you suppose Charlie has lost the power of speech, is that normal in cases like this?" asked Abbie.

"I have no idea," said Mavis. "I don't think the nurse knew herself, but no doubt the doctor or consultant has some idea. I don't suppose the notion of putting people into or bringing them out of a coma is particularly widespread. I don't suppose that before the onset of this Covid pandemic, that they would use it as a normal procedure?"

Abbie nodded in agreement. "I know," she said. "I saw that there was a husband of a breakfast TV presenter who suffered badly from a strain of Covid which affected him so seriously that he remained in a coma for almost nine months, and when he did come out of the coma he was not anywhere near normal and remains almost bed bound which is of course nowhere near a full recovery."

"Yes," agreed Mavis. "I was thinking about that situation when I saw Charlie this morning. There was a blankness behind his eyes which I didn't like the look of. Anyway, I will probably find out later today, I will pop in and see him on my way home this afternoon."

And so it was that later that afternoon, Mavis was in the ward where Charlie was lying quietly in his bed, with Des seated beside him. As she approached, Mavis raised her eyebrows in a silent but hopeful enquiry but Des, in response gave a half-hearted grimace.

"No improvement then?" suggested Mavis.

Des shook his head grimly. "Nah," he offered pessimistically. "He is just not himself, and does not seem to have come back to us complete. They are considering matters at the moment but don't have anything positive to say for now. I fear that he may never come back to us as his old self."

Mavis grasped Charlie's hand and whispered her 'hello' to him and squeezed the hand but felt not even the faintest response. The eyes, as on the previous day, looked blank.

"I have to get home, I did not tell George that I would be late, please contact me if there is any change."

Des nodded, and Mavis gave Charlie's hand another squeeze before making her way out of the ward. When she got home George was making a spaghetti Bolognese. The meaty sauce was simmering in the pan and the pasta had just been deposited into a large saucepan of boiling water. Together they laid the kitchen table, and the meals were served upon plates and George grated some parmesan cheese over both. As they sat down to eat Mavis told him of the progress, or rather the lack of progress, in Charlie's medical recovery.

Chapter 56

Abbie had been quite shocked by the news that Charlie was suffering severely from problems connected with the Covid virus that he had contracted somewhere recently. She reflected that since Charlie was at present unconscious in a hospital bed, it was just as well that he had managed to complete his report about the disappearance of the money at the security firm. Having had that thought she was immediately overcome with guilt at having such a thought.

She had had a busy day which included her usual early start due since it was her college day. She had been pleased to meet Mavis of course but was not gratified to hear about Charlie's condition in his hospital bed. Before the lecture started and during the lunch hour the girls had time for a chat primarily about poor Charlie. Over lunch Mavis informed her of the fact that Charlie remained in a coma but the hope was that he would soon be brought out of the coma and be his old self again. Once their lunch time ended they had to get back to the subject of the tort of Nuisance. When the lecture was finished Mavis announced that she would be re-visiting Charlie in hospital on her way home.

Abbie for her part, went straight home and found her mother in the kitchen just retrieving from the oven a steak and kidney pie which she had made earlier. The potatoes and vegetables were simmering in separate saucepans.

"Aah," said Stephanie as Abbie walked in. "You are just in time, I was just making the gravy. What sort of day have you had?"

Abbie told her about her day and in particular about the condition of Charlie in hospital.

"He is still in an induced coma but the hospital are going to bring him back to consciousness and we will all keep our fingers crossed about that."

They both settled down to enjoy their pie and had a good gossip about all sorts of things. Abbie told her that her friend Joyce would be calling round to see her that evening. Soon after they had finished their meal the doorbell rang, and Joyce was admitted into their kitchen lounge area. She spent a half hour chatting with Stephanie and then she and Abbie made their way upstairs to Abbie's bedroom to chat together.

"So," asked Abbie. "How are things going with Carlos?"

Joyce explained that there had not been sufficient time for her and Carlos to spend time together. Apparently, Carlos had had so many exercise sessions in the last week or so that he had not been able to spare any time to meet Joyce. Abbie had a strong feeling that her friend was slightly disappointed but could not complain because of the popularity of his classes.

"It seems," she said with a chuckle. "That the only way I am ever going to spend time with him is to join his classes."

Abbie was sceptical about that but did not pass any judgement. She hoped that her friend would not be disappointed by the lack of attention from Carlos and that this development did not indicate a waning of the Spaniard's affection for Joyce. Her friend eagerly asked her to give her all the details of her recent meeting with Pete the plumber.

"Well," she said and paused for a moment. "I spoke to you on the telephone while I was there. I was on the deck of his boat at the time. It is an elderly sailing boat which, although he spends lots of time on it (painting and maintaining it regularly), still looks run-down and worn out. He came up on deck when I finished talking to you, and had just decided that, as there was not a single drop of breeze to sail with, we would go instead down the road to his local pub, which turned out to be quite nice. We took a table in the garden and had a delicious meal and a drink and long chat. He is a lovely man, much nicer than I expected, and I really enjoyed the time that we spent together."

"But," interjected Joyce.

"But," resumed Abbie. "Although he was clearly a lovely chap, I soon realized that he and I would not be suitable to be a couple. He was obviously totally in love with his children, and I suspect, still possibly in love with his wife, and spoke of little else. But nothing he said about them was in any way bitter or complaining. He was simply too nice to be by himself and I* felt so sad for him. Although he had joined the dating site, he was not really looking for a new partner. He simply wanted the old one back, but she had chosen someone else with whom she now lived along with his children. I felt so sorry for him; it was truly tragic. He clearly wanted his old life back but that was never going to happen. I was certainly not prepared to try to imitate his former wife or try to be a stepmother to his children, so I will not be seeing him again."

"So" concluded Joyce dismally, "your first adventure on the dating site has not ended perfectly, But would you consider trying again?"

"Well," said Abbie "I guess I would. I was not disappointed with Pete. As I said, he was a beautiful man, but he was not looking for me, he was searching for a duplicate of his lost wife. I felt disappointed for him rather than with him."

Chapter 57

It had been a busy day for Des. He had appeared in the Magistrate's court in the morning giving evidence in a case against a motorist who had injured a pedestrian in a shopping area. The street had a speed limit of twenty miles an hour and an elderly gentleman was knocked down by the motorist at a pedestrian crossing area. Ordinarily, if evidence was being offered by a police officer it would have required a patrol car driver as a witness. By coincidence, Des was a witness in the car behind the motorist and had taken charge of the situation as soon as it occurred. The motorist was charged with negligent driving, although the pedestrian was thankfully not seriously injured. The motorist had pleaded not guilty to the charge and so the Crown Prosecution had insisted that Des appeared in court to give evidence.

Des himself could not understand why the matter had gone to trial since it was, he thought, an open and shut case, but perhaps the accused had hoped that somehow, he could avoid losing his driving licence by taking part in a spirited defence in the local court. However, the motorist was found guilty and the only compensation, as far as Des was concerned, was that he was able to return to his office within the hour.

He thought however that since the trial had been shorter than expected, and since he would not be expected back at the office for a couple of hours, he would utilise the spare time afforded to him by visiting Charlie in hospital and hope to track down the consultant, or at least the Registrar he had seen before to try to get some common sense out of them and some prediction as to his friend's chances of recovering soon. He hoped that a visit during the daytime rather than at the end of the working day might produce more positive information.

When he arrived at the hospital he was surprised to find Mavis sitting next to Charlie's bed and weeping quietly.

"Aaw, what's the news?" he enquired concerned by her obvious dismay.

"Oh Des" she muttered indicating the detective lying in his bed with a fixed stare and a dribble of saliva dripping from one side of his mouth. As if to emphasise the situation she wiped his mouth with a tissue. "He has been like this for an hour. There is nothing there. He is not with us and doesn't look like he ever will be. I'm scared Des and no one seems to know what is going to happen to him."

"That's why I came here this morning." Said Des decisively, "just wait here will you, I'm going to see if I can find someone who will give us an answer."

Mavis remained by the bedside still despairing at the countenance of Charlie. She took another tissue from her handbag and wiped away the spittle from his lip and while doing this she looked closely into his eyes from a close distance. She whispered his name directly into his nearest ear and watched his eye for any reaction. She noted that there was not any positive reaction from him. She realized that although his eyes were open, his brain was not functioning properly if at all.

Des returned a few moments later accompanied by the Registrar whom he had met a day or two ago. The young man examined Charlie and the medical notes at the end of his bed. He shook his head mournfully and said,

"I am sorry, but there has been no improvement in your friend's condition."

"But what are the chances of him making a full recovery?" asked Des.

The young Registrar shook his head and said,

"I have absolutely no idea. It could be tomorrow, next week, or next year or never."

"Do you mean to say that he might stay like this for ever?" asked Mavis, "that surely cannot be the case. There must be something you can do?"

The young man looked sympathetic but still looked unable to help,

"I will not mislead you," he said carefully picking his words, "we just simply don't know why he is not responding. We have no historic experience of this disease to learn from and therefore can only keep our eye on him and hope that there might be a breakthrough which may occur of its own device. We do not know why he has not responded."

The registrar expressed his sympathy to them both and took his leave of them. Mavis and Des were left with a problem which neither of them could feel any blame in respect thereof. They both knew that there was no definite likelihood of Charlie making an early recovery.

"Well " said Des, "I do know that Charlie has a police pension which he receives. It is not a full pension because he did not serve the necessary length of service, but it would provide a small kitty which might be used to put towards the fees of a nursing home where he could be looked after pending a possible recovery."

Mavis looked firmly into the middle distance and grimaced,

"I think I will have to have a chat with George tonight and see where we can go with this problem."

Chapter 58

Mavis arrived home the evening before and decided that she could not face the conversation she knew she must have with her husband before going to bed. She felt so exhausted and preferred to leave it until the morning.

Accordingly she arose early the following morning and showered and dressed before George awoke and went down to the kitchen dining area and was making herself some cereal for her breakfast. She poured a glass of orange juice and sat down to consume it when George walked into the room wearing just a pair of boxer shorts.

"How are you my darling?" he asked kissing her affectionately on the neck from behind. "You're up early again."

"I know," agreed Mavis. "I have lots to do at work today, I didn't want to start too late."

"You slept so soundly last night, I never got the chance to ask you. How was Charlie when you saw him yesterday?"

"No better I'm afraid there was no change. His eyes are open but there is nothing behind the stare. He cannot speak or communicate in any way. The hospital are clueless as to why and are simply hoping that he might recover but I can tell you it does not look as though there will be nay recovery."

She started to weep quietly, "He cannot stay in hospital for ever, and if there is no eventual recovery he will have to go into a nursing home which can offer expert medical attention. I did not want to say anything to Des but he was talking about a partial pension which Charlie has from when he was a policeman. I think he knows that the small pension will not pay for expert medical attention but I did not want to promise any of your money to look after him, but I remember when I was threatened by one of the twins, Charlie stepped between me and him and nearly got himself killed on my behalf." She was crying openly now and shuddered with grief.

George hugged her and said resolutely to her, "My darling, how many times do I have to tell you? It is not my money, it is our money. I only inherited it, I did not earn it. Since we got married, it is as much your money as it is mine. I have known Charlie about as long as I have known you. If he needs medical attention then we will pay for it as long as is necessary."

Mavis burst into another fit of crying and wrapped her arms around him and whispered, "Thank you so much, you are so brilliant and I love you so much."

"Listen," said George. "You do not have to run everything past me for every penny you spend. It is as much your money as mine, understand?"

Mavis nodded again and thanked him once more.

"Good," he said firmly. "That's settled then. I've just finished that final bedroom, so I have nothing in particular to do today, so I will research on suitable Nursing homes for Charlie today, and absolutely no rubbish. Nothing but the best for Charlie; and for as long as it takes, OK?"

Mavis hugged him again and whispered in his ear, "I just don't know what I did to deserve you."

"Likewise," responded George. "You are all I have ever wanted."

Mavis embraced him once more and said, "You're too much, I want your baby George." They both kissed sensually until Mavis disentangled herself and said she was going to work.

Chapter 59

Des was in his office finishing off a report. He completed the last word on the last page and felt some relief as he printed off the pages and tapped them upon his desk to put them in order like a pack of cards. As he did this there was a knock on his door and his sergeant walked in carrying some papers. He sat down in the chair opposite Des and threw the papers on the desk between them.

"You'll never guess," he said with an air of extreme frustration. "Our colleagues in Australia have made enquiries of the Commonwealth bank and the account has been emptied."

"Really?" enquired Des, his eyes raised. "Where did it go?"

"That's just it," said the sergeant with even more frustration in his voice. "Nobody knows. The account was emptied by somebody, but no one knows who, or where it went."

"What!" raged Des. "Are you saying that those country bumpkins out there have no record of who withdrew the money and where it went? No camera record from the bank? No photograph of anyone?"

"Exactly," replied the sergeant. "The end of the trail."

"Well, I'm blessed," said Des in complete outrage. "So the slimy little shyster, who stole from just about everyone he came across, has got away from every channel of law enforcement and is probably, even as we speak, making his way to Hong Kong or mainland China?"

The sergeant nodded sagely and said, "That is about the size of it. I honestly don't believe we will ever see any trace of him or hear anything further about him again. I am certain that he will never return to this country."

"Shit!" exclaimed Des still feeling guilty and frustrated. "This is a bloody outrage. Everything has gone pear-shaped and although no one, except for Jones himself, has done anything deliberately wrong overall, everyone has made a complete pig's ear of everything. The only one who could not be faulted is Charlie, and he is currently in a coma in a hospital bed. How ironic is that? A total injustice!"

"Well," said the Sergeant rising from his chair. "I guess the only compensation was the fact that most of the stolen money has been recovered."

Des nodded philosophically and reflected that his Sergeant was probably right. His mind moved to Charlie, and he wondered how his old friend would be when he visited him at the end of the day.

Mavis had had a busy day and, quite unlike her, she had been relieved to finish the day on time and hurry home to see George who she found in the kitchen immersed in a Bolognese sauce. When she walked in, he instantly put a saucepan on the boil to accommodate the spaghetti. She gave him a kiss and asked what sort of day he had had.

"Hmm," he offered with an upward lilt of his voice. "Pretty good thanks. I found a suitable nursing home for Charlie."

"Oh really," cried Mavis with glee. "How did you manage to do that?"

"Oh, quite easy really," responded George. "I spoke on the phone with Pete, and he directed me to a home which is run by the father and mother of a guy in the rugby club. They are called Mr and Mrs Sand. The name of the home is 'Sandy Homes' and it is just up the road from here. It is a former Victorian mansion which has been altered and re-decorated into the best nursing home in town according to Pete. I'll take you up there after dinner and show you the outside."

"Oh, thank you so much my darling. And thank you Pete, I suppose," said Mavis.

They ate their spaghetti Bolognese which George had cooked and Mavis told him it was delicious. She also told him how serious she considered the condition of Charlie was, and how grateful she was that he (George), had agreed to finance the nursing home fees for the detective until he recovered.

"You do realize darling that he might never recover consciousness and could remain in a coma for the rest of his life."

"So be it," replied George. "Charlie is our friend ,and he probably saved your life that time the twin lost his temper. We can afford it and we owe it to him to make sure he gets all the help he needs."

Mavis leaned across the table and gave him a kiss.

"You are just so brilliant darling," she said.

They both cleared away their plates and then George said, "Come on, then I'll show you where Sandy Homes is."

They stepped outside and jumped in their car and George drove up the hill behind their home and parked outside the converted mansion which had a signpost outside it which read 'Sandy Homes' Mavis looked at the luxurious property and was satisfied that Charlie would almost certainly get the best possible attention therein. She liked the look of the verandas outside each room.

"I think it looks perfect darling, and thanks again. Now, if you don't mind, I would like to pop down to the hospital and check on Charlie. I know that Des will be with him, so I want to tell him the arrangements we have made about Charlie's future."

"Sure," said George. He put the car in gear and drove them to the hospital. When they arrived at the ward in which Charlie was housed. As Mavis had predicted, Des was by his bed. They both explained to him the arrangements they had made for Charlie's immediate and/or long -term future. Des and George both went off to find a member of staff to make the announcement and arrangements for the transfer of Charlie to Sandy Homes. Mavis sat down beside the prostrate detective and gripped his hand and gave it a squeeze. Charlie opened his eyes and gazed at her. There was something about the look in his eyes that was less distant and vacant compared to the robotic stare she had become used to. She leaned forward towards him and whispered, "Hello, Charlie."

His eyes no longer stared ahead in a fixed, mechanical way. Instead, as she leaned forward towards him, she saw his eyes descend to her cleavage and the curl of his lips break into a faint smile.

She smiled back broadly and said with tears in her eyes,

"Welcome back, Charlie."

The End